John Blayne looked at Kate standing there in her incredible maid's costume. He put his hands in his pockets to keep them safe and sauntered toward her.

"I have an idea. *You* can help me!"

She looked at him, her face shining with laughter. "*Can* isn't the question. It's *will* I—"

"Persuade Sir Richard to let me have the castle, Kate—and you with it!"

"Me—like a piece of furniture?"

She had stopped laughing.

"I could never get the castle together again without you," he said. "You can be a special consultant or something—anything you like."

She drew back a step.

"I'll pay you," he said, following her.

"Pay me?" she repeated. "I'm not for sale . . . any more than the castle is."

She walked away from him across the dim room to the window. He kept his distance, watching her. How strange she was! Who was she?

He came to her side and saw her face, pale and beautiful and remote. Whoever she was, he knew now he could never forget her.

DEATH IN THE CASTLE
was originally published by
The John Day Company, Inc.

Pearl S. Buck

Death in the Castle

A POCKET BOOK EDITION published by
Simon & Schuster of Canada, Ltd. • Markham, Ontario, Canada
Registered User of the Trademark

DEATH IN THE CASTLE

John Day edition published 1965

POCKET BOOK edition published May, 1967
9th printing .... January, 1976

This POCKET BOOK edition includes every word contained
in the original, higher-priced edition. It is printed from
brand-new plates made from completely reset, clear, easy-
to-read type. POCKET BOOK editions are published by
POCKET BOOKS, a division of Simon & Schuster of Canada,
Ltd., 330 Steelcase Road, Markham, Ontario L3R 2M1.
Trademarks registered in Canada and other countries.

Standard Book Number: 671-80327-1.
Printed in Canada.

Author's Note

EVERY book tells two stories: one concerns the characters, the other the author, and how he happened to write such a book. *Death in the Castle* began some years ago in England. With Tad Danielewski, my partner in Stratton Productions, I visited a beautiful ancient castle. Out of its hoary shadows and castellated towers the characters emerged, fictitious and yet so strangely vivid that their story unfolded in my mind in an instant.

Since Tad Danielewski is a stage and screen director, we immediately fell into a discussion of how their story was to be presented. He thought in film, I thought in novel. We decided upon a cooperative effort. I wrote the novel, he wrote the screenplay. The work went on almost simultaneously.

Perhaps the reader will find the same enchantment that I experienced when the story took shape, as if in double exposure—one faithfully echoing the other, promising a new kind of excitement generated by the magic of the screen and the participating audience.

The purpose of art is communication, but in the arts each uses its own means, and each gains its own response. In the novel the reader is required to exert his creative imagination in order to participate. In the film participation is more direct and less subjective, for the viewer feels that he is actively transported into the scene itself.

We bring you both: now the novel, a little later the film, of *Death in the Castle*.

—PEARL S. BUCK

Death in the

in the

Castle

Part One

~~~

THE delicate sunshine of an English spring shone through the tall and mullioned windows of the castle. He had been up since dawn, on horseback as he was every morning, riding about the farm while she slept. By the time he had cantered home it was half past nine and he was hungry. He had tramped into the dining hall where they had all their meals, except tea. She talked sometimes of a breakfast room, but he was accustomed from his earliest memory to this enormous room and the long table beneath the chandelier where they now sat, he at the north end and she at the south.

This morning, however, she had been up earlier than usual. How else could the bowl of daffodils on the table be explained? They lifted their yellow trumpets, three or four dozen of them, in a big silver bowl on the lace mat. Unless Kate had got into the garden? Years ago they had decided not to talk at breakfast, though the decision had been forgotten more often than not. She had even complained because he expected her, a young bride, to eat breakfast with him. He could see her yet, a slip of a girl, an English beauty, blue eyes under honey-colored hair, facing him across the distance. He could hear her high sweet voice, complaining and willful.

"It's such a beastly time of day, Richard! My parents never wanted to see each other so early."

"My dear," he had retorted, laughing. "If I had been compelled to face your mother every morning I might have felt the same. She is a Gorgon but you're not. You've a face like a rose, Mary, and I want to see it across my breakfast kidney and bacon. It's my prerogative."

"All the same, I shan't talk," she had threatened while her eyes smiled.

"You needn't," he had said, and through the thirty-five years of their happy marriage she had been very nearly silent in the morning, though faithfully breakfasting with him. Stubborn little thing!

He looked at the rose of a face now, across the table. It was still pretty, a slightly faded rose, perhaps, but worth looking at, and not at all what her mother's had been—more like her father's perhaps, a gentle peer retiring too early to a crumbling Cornwall fortress of a castle. He had merely brought her from one castle to another, except that he had not allowed this castle to crumble and never would, in spite of these preposterous times when one was to be penalized, it seemed, for having been born in one's family seat.

She caught his half-frowning glance over the daffodils and lifted her eyebrows to inquire.

"Nothing," he said abruptly, "just remembering an odd moment."

Wells, who was both cook and butler in these lean days, had been standing with his back to them, facing the buffet; he now broke an egg into hot water. She liked her egg poached, with a side serving of kippered herring. Wells, tall and erect in a worn gray uniform, was bone thin with age; his white hair was brushed carefully, his hands were still steady. He had been footman when Sir Richard was a boy and Lady Mary a small fair-haired girl in short white frocks. They were enchanted enemies in those days, he and she, their families distant neighbors, and Mary had pretended not to see Richard when he came with his mother to tea and showed off with handsprings and gymnastics when the two of them were sent out to play on the lawn.

Wells turned to reveal a long and melancholy face. "Will you have an egg this morning, Sir Richard? With your kidney and bacon?"

"I will, thanks," he replied. "I daresay I'll need it. Is Kate gone to the station yet?"

"It's a bit early, sir. She's just dusting the great hall, preparatory to the American, sir."

"Go and tell her she'll be late."

"Yes, Sir Richard."

The old man left the room, coping bravely with a slight limp. Silence fell. Lady Mary drank her tea, gazing reflectively at the daffodils. Sir Richard buttered his toast and glanced at her.

"I say, my dear, you'll meet with us, you know."

For a moment he thought she would not break her silence. Then she spoke, her voice still high and sweet and oddly youthful with the hair now white.

"I hadn't thought I should. Must I?"

"I shan't want to meet him alone," he said.

"Did you telephone Philip Webster?"

"By Jove, I forgot!" He leapt to his feet and was halfway to the door when she spoke again.

"I telephoned him."

He paused. "What? I say, that was good of you! I don't know why I forgot—"

"You won't need me if he's here."

"Yes, I shall. Moral support. Webster's such a pessimist—convinced the worst will happen, and I am too easily convinced."

He sat down again. Somehow once the conversation

was begun, he wanted to keep it going. "It was Webster who thought of this business with the American. He'll push me. He'll tell me the country is doomed and the castle with it and all that rot."

She poured a second cup of tea. "Why he should have found the American, of all people! Perhaps it was because your father sold the two paintings from the ballroom to an American the year we were married. But that was so long ago! Remember? To pay for our honeymoon tour, I'm afraid, poor dear!"

"I paid for the honeymoon," Sir Richard said flatly. It was the ballrooms he paid for. "Everything for the land, in those days," he went on, grumbling. "He scrimped me to the bone at Oxford. A lot of good it did! The land was never better, but it's still not enough, unless we modernize. And taxes! I thought when we let the damned public come in we might be saved. Nothing is enough, it seems. Government wants everything."

She spread marmalade on a bit of toast. "Yes, it was the paintings reminded Philip. Fancy his resorting to an American otherwise!"

He was suddenly irritable. The pounding headache, to which he had become liable in the last year, had attacked him again. "Stop complaining about what I cannot help," he said sharply.

Out in the hall Wells stood in disapproval of his granddaughter. "Kate, you're wanted. They think you'll be late."

"Yes, Granddad, just one more minute, please."

She was dusting the cabinet of heavy oak, English oak, carved with the royal arms. Five hundred years the castle had been the home of royalty and then it had been given to the Sedgeley family, and another five hundred years had passed. Kate dreamed through the centuries while she worked day after day, remembering the books she had pored over in the library during the years she had been growing up in the castle. They had spoiled her, Sir Richard and Lady Mary, making a pet of her and then sending her to school in London, when her grandfather was only the butler. They had spoiled her as they had her father, Colin, who had grown up in the castle too. He had refused to go properly into service as footman under his father; instead he had run off to London, had been an artist for awhile, then when the war came along joined the Air Force and got himself trained as a pilot.

All in one year Colin had married, become a war hero, and been killed in an air raid on London the very day he had been given leave to see his newborn daughter. Kate's mother had been killed too, and the baby had been saved only because someone had had the wit to push her in her basket under a kitchen table.

An orphan at the age of nine days, Kate had been brought back to the castle by her grandfather. Wells was all she had known in the way of parents, for her grandmother, Elsie Wells, had died when Colin was born. As for Kate's mother's side of the family, nothing was ever said. Kate early learned that there were some things about which one did not speak; questions were not asked for answers would not be forthcoming.

Her grandfather had brought her up well, teaching her what he knew and training her in the old ways; but there had come a time when Sir Richard and Lady Mary—Sir Richard especially—had insisted that Kate have more education than the village school could give, so she had been sent to London. Wells did not approve, but there was nothing he could say or do against Sir Richard. Kate had been glad to go. In London she had learned new ways of usefulness. She could drive the car now when Sir Richard wanted her to; she could help Lady Mary with her correspondence. She was considerably more than a servant, considerably less than a daughter; but the castle was her home.

What her life might have been without the shelter of the castle she could not guess; what her life, and her grandfather's too, might be if the castle were no longer to be home was something she would not think about.

"You're working too hard," Wells said as he sat down heavily in a huge oak chair, King Charles's chair. He sat nowadays whenever he could, even for a moment.

Kate went on dusting the intricate details of the table, a long slab of polished wood set upon iron legs and claw feet holding balls of crystal.

"Not really," she said cheerfully. "I like working about, Granddad."

"You're as headstrong as your father," Wells said, but his tone had more pride than criticism in it. "I could do nothing with Colin from the moment he was born. And when he married above his station—"

She interrupted. "Now, Granddad, you've told me that over and over, and I've far too much on my mind now to listen again to that old story."

He got to his feet. "You're Miss Bossy, as usual, and have been since you were born. You take after your dad all right. You'd better get yourself into the hall, or—"

He moved slowly toward the door but Kate flew ahead of him and was in the great hall before he was.

"Good morning, Sir Richard. Grandfather says you called me?"

She saw as she talked that his cup was empty and she took it from the table to the buffet and filled it with hot coffee, hot milk and two lumps of sugar, moving deftly and swiftly, a small alert figure.

"You'll be late," Sir Richard grumbled, accepting the service.

"Take off your apron, Kate," Lady Mary directed.

She took it off. "Yes, my lady. I'm quite ready, as you see—a clean blouse and my tweed skirt. I've only to slip on my jacket and brush my hair back."

"I say you'll be late," Sir Richard repeated.

She smiled at him, coaxing, her brown hair curling about her vivid face.

"Sir Richard, dear, I will not be late. I know how long it takes."

"You always drive too fast, you young rascal—"

"Ah no, I don't, sir. I'm that careful you wouldn't believe—"

"You're what I wouldn't believe. You do everything too fast."

"Have I ever had a smash?"

"You've never had to drive an American before."

Kate laughed. "You make it sound as though he weren't human!"

"I'm not sure of the breed!"

They had been talking as equals, a young woman and an older man, and Sir Richard enjoyed it. She knew from habit, however, exactly when to slip from the role of almost daughter to almost maid, and she did so now.

"Please, Sir Richard, how will I know the American when I see him?"

"How should I know? I've never seen him myself."

Lady Mary interrupted, but mild and detached as usual. "He'll be the only one who doesn't look an Englishman, I daresay."

Kate laughed again, a pleasant ready music, rippling with gaiety. "Perhaps I'll coax him back on the train again to America! Or, if I don't like his looks, I'll tell him about the Duke's bedroom and properly frighten him."

Sir Richard put down his cup. "He should be in King John's room. We must show him our best."

"Too damp," Lady Mary said. "There's that drip in the left corner of the ceiling where the plaster fell. Years ago it was, and it still drips. I can't think why. Wells, why don't you know?"

"Nobody has ever known, my lady."

"Ah well, it can't matter now, since the castle's to be sold, it seems—unless some one thinks of something."

"It's a crime, my lady—asking your pardon." Wells said.

Sir Richard pounded his fist on the table. "Kate!"

Kate had been looking from one face to the other, her eyes questioning, her lips parted, and she gave a start at the sound of his voice. "I am gone, sir," she breathed and was gone.

They were silent again until Wells, faltering at the buffet and clattering nervously the silver dishes, turned to them, trembling with emotion, which he knew they would not allow him to reveal.

"If that's all, sir, I'd better be getting into the kitchen. The butcher boy will be wanting me. A small roast for tonight, my lady?"

Lady Mary nodded indifferently, and he went away. They had finished eating. Sir Richard lit his pipe and she watched him, meditating, her silvery head held a little to the left. It was she who broke the silence, her voice plaintively firm.

"We haven't tried everything, you know, Richard—not really, I mean."

He puffed twice. "Can you think of something? I can't. Lucky that Webster found those letters in the files! The Blaynes are enormously wealthy. Oil, I believe, or it may be steel, but Americans are full of oil."

"Hateful stuff! Black smoke in all their cities, I'm told. No wonder they want to hang their paintings here. Will they bring back the two they took away?"

"My dear, they'll do whatever they like with the two paintings—they paid for them. Otherwise we'd have no bathrooms in the castle. Besides, that was so long ago."

"Five bathrooms for twenty-seven bedrooms!"

"Better than the maids with rubber tubs and jugs of

hot water, as it was when I was a lad. Gad, I'll never forget the way those rubber tubs could sag and spill the water through the ceiling! I let it happen the morning the Prince of Wales was here and the water came through on this table. I was only seventeen and I very nearly died of shame—wouldn't come down to breakfast and my father—"

She interrupted with gentle laughter. "Richard, really! You told me about it the first day we met—and how many times since!"

"It's a good story, however often I tell it," he retorted.

They heard the honking of a horn as he spoke. Together they rose and went out into the courtyard. The old Rolls Royce stood there bravely, trembling under the throbbing engine. At the wheel, all the windows down, Kate sat enthroned, her dark hair flying in short curls about her face.

"I'm off," she cried.

Standing side by side, very straight and gallant, they nodded and waved, looking after her as she drove away.

. . . The darlings, she thought, as she sped through the summer green along the drive, the brave old darlings, giving up their treasure, their heritage, their home, their castle! My home, too, she reminded herself, though her claim was far different from theirs. If the American wasn't moved at the sight of them, if he didn't say at once that he simply couldn't bear to put them out, if he destroyed her dream of their living on exactly as they always had, only with the paintings on the walls if the castle was to be a museum, but everything else just as it was, and she looking after it all as she did now, if he didn't see how impossible, how cruel, any change would be, then she would—she would simply hate him, that was all. She would hate him with all her heart and she would manage somehow to spoil everything, she would indeed.

She looked back before the next rise of land should take the castle from her view; she leaned out of the window dangerously far for that last glimpse she always sought. How beautiful the castle was in the sunlight! Sir Richard and La————————————t where they had been w————————— shining on their white h————————————for them to whom the cas————————————elonged, too, in a way. S————————————omething high above ther————————————ad took them from her s——

Lady Mary's————————————w under the high overha——

"Richard, do you see something up there?"

"Where?"

"The lost window. Someone's there—"

"How can it be lost if someone's there?"

"It might be *they*."

"Oh, come now, my dear!"

"Ah, but you never say whether you really believe or don't believe."

"What is there to believe?"

"You know quite well."

"What?"

"Richard, you're being stupid. It's naughty of you!"

"To tell you the truth, then—I don't see anything at the window—I never do."

She stamped her foot at this and stooped to a bed of the daffodils, yellow against the gray stone of the castle. He gazed down, tender-eyed, at her slight figure and the silvery hair. His headache was gone as suddenly as it had come and he felt immense relief.

"Am I being stupid, my love? Perhaps! But who knows anything these days? I'd sooner believe you than anyone else."

She reached for his hand at that and they walked to

the great yews, clipped in the shape of elephants. There they paused in mutual gloom for the yews had been planted two hundred years ago and clipped a hundred years later by a Sedgeley who had seen service in India.

"He'll chop down the elephants, that American," she said.

"Nonsense. Americans aren't savages nowadays."

"You talk sometimes as though they were."

"That's because I don't relish having them in my castle or cutting down my yews."

They walked on to the rose garden. Impatient bees were fretting over the buds not yet ready to bloom.

She was brooding over the roses. "He won't know about roses, I daresay. I've never heard of American roses."

"Nor I. I daresay they can't grow roses in their beastly climate."

"Will he chew gum?"

"Spare me these clichés, my dear. He's probably a decent sort, in which case he'll not chew gum. At least he knows paintings."

"Where'll he have his meals? I shan't be able to talk if he's at table with us."

"Wells can take him a tray."

As though at the mention of his name, Wells appeared. "A man has arrived, Sir Richard, in a motorcar," he announced in a sepulchral voice.

Sir Richard looked at him with irritation. "But the castle is closed today. It's only Tuesday."

"I told him so, sir," Wells said.

"Very well—then tell him again. It doesn't pay to have fewer than ten people on a tour through the castle. Tell him so."

"He's the persistent sort, sir," Wells said doubtfully.

Sir Richard rubbed his nose. "Then tell him to come on Thursday with the rest of the public."

"It's an American motorcar, sir."

Lady Mary entered the conversation with an air of solving the problem. "Ask his chauffeur who he is."

"He's driving himself, my lady."

"Ah, well then," she said decisively. "He's a tourist or he's selling something. If the former, tell him he can't see the castle today and we make no exceptions. If the latter, tell him to apply at the service door and then meet him there and send him away."

"Yes, my lady." Wells bowed slightly and left them.

They watched him sadly. "One of these days," Sir Richard began—

She cut him off. "Don't say it, Richard. I can't think what we'll do without Wells. He's like the castle. I've thought of things, of course, finding a husband for Kate, for example—someone who could help Wells, you know, until—and perhaps be a sort of chef man while—"

She was surprised at Sir Richard's look of horror.

"Impossible!"

"What do you mean, Richard?"

"A husband for Kate—someone like—*Wells?*"

"I don't see why not—"

"Kate married to a butler sort of—cook?"

"Really, Richard, she's only a maid—a very wonderful one and so on, but—why do you look at me like that?"

"I don't think of her as a maid—"

"Richard, you're being very odd—"

"I'm not being odd, my dear. It's just that I can't bear to think of life's being different than it's always been for us. We're not getting younger and it'll be difficult, at best—"

He turned away abruptly. She went to his side and laid her cheek against his sleeve.

"Ah, Richard, don't grieve! Do you know what I'm thinking of? The first day you kissed me—remember? In

spring—a day like this—and the daffodils blooming, too.
And your mother came out—"

Sir Richard put his arm about her shoulders. "By Jove,
I'd forgotten! She said, 'You did that rather nicely, my
son.' "

"I could have wept, I was so shy!"

"And I said—"

She interrupted. "Richard, there must be something
we can do to save the castle! Life's gone on here for a
thousand years—how can it stop with us? What have
we done?"

"What haven't we done?" he said sadly. "It's nothing
we can help. It's the end of an age, my love, and we end
with it, that's all. Someone has to, I suppose—someone
had to even when Rome fell. Our castle is built on
Roman ruins, you know. There's no alternative now, I'm
afraid—"

"Are you sure Webster has done all he can?"

"He showed me the letters he'd had—two possibilities,
that's all. Government would buy the castle for a prison,
that's bad enough but the other is worse—the atomic
people want to pull it down and build a plant here. They
need a bit of a desert, and our five thousand acres of
forest and farm would do nicely."

She shuddered and sat down on a low rock wall. "Oh
no—"

He felt for his pipe and tobacco pouch, filled the pipe,
lit it and drew hard. "Well, my dear, all that's left is to
keep on with the farm, and that we can't, it seems, without selling the castle. The tenants complain about leak-
ing roofs and no modern improvements and I don't know
where to look for the money for that sort of thing. No,
the museum's best. We'll turn it over to the American
and retire to the gatehouse. It will be comfortable
enough, I daresay. And the money he gives us will pay
for the farm improvements and perhaps we can make do

in our time, God willing. At least the castle won't be a prison for criminals—or be demolished."

She pushed back her short white hair.

"I wish you wouldn't mention God. . . . If we'd had a son—"

"We haven't," he said shortly.

"But if we had, could he—"

"My dear, why do you speak of him when he was never born or even conceived, for that matter? We settled that long ago."

"You still think it was my fault!"

He knocked the ash out of his pipe. "Damn this thing —it won't draw."

She continued, her voice slightly belligerent. "You know, Richard, it was never settled that I was the one at fault. It was very unkind of you not to be willing to go and have yourself examined."

He turned on her. "Now why do you bring that up again? It's absurd—at our age. And I—there was no reason to think that I—besides, I suggested that we adopt a child."

She moved away from him. "You know very well that adopted children can't inherit. It has to be your issue."

"Male issue," he retorted. "It could have been an adopted daughter. Fact is"—he was working at his pipe again, cleaning it with a bit of stick he plucked from a shrub—"fact is, I've thought once or twice of adopting Kate."

"Kate? Ah, that's why you say she's not like a maid!"

"It's too late now, I suppose."

"Much too late," she said with decision.

They heard at this moment the halting clatter of the old car. Kate was coming back. The car turned into the gate at the end of the driveway and stopped.

"The damned thing has stalled," Sir Richard said anxiously. He waited, watching while Kate stepped down from the high old vehicle. Four men followed her, all in dark suits and carrying briefcases.

"Good God," Sir Richard muttered.

"Richard," Lady Mary said under her breath. "I feel faint—"

"Nonsense! Keep a stiff upper lip, my dear. The American has brought his minions. But I wish Webster were here."

He went forward, his tall lean frame erect. "Good morning, which one of you is Mr. John Blayne?"

"None of them, Sir Richard," Kate said. The wind was blowing her curly hair about her face and she looked vexed. "He's coming by motorcar."

The men came forward one by one and Sir Richard felt his hand wrenched four times. Lady Mary stood behind him, her hands safely clasped. The youngest one spoke brightly, a trim fellow with sandy hair in a crew cut.

"Mr. Blayne left London right after breakfast, sir. He's driving himself."

"He'll probably lose his way, which he does at the drop of a hat," a second young man said briskly.

Sir Richard looked from one to the other. They were all alike, all clean and dapper with hair in crew cuts, all alarmingly healthy and efficient-looking.

"Mr. Blayne," said the third quietly, "is always stopping to look at cathedrals and such. Probably he'll get here tomorrow at the earliest."

"Shall we get started?" the fourth asked Sir Richard.

"Started?" Sir Richard repeated.

"Yes, on the castle. That's why we're here. Mr. Blayne doesn't like us to waste any time."

They were interrupted by Wells, jogging in a trot from behind the yews and gasping for breath. "He's lost, sir!" he cried in a thin shriek.

"Control yourself, Wells," Sir Richard said sternly.

"Stop running. Breathe deeply twice and then speak like a rational creature."

"Really, Wells," Lady Mary supplemented. "You'll have an apoplexy and then what'll we do? So inconsiderate of you!"

"Grandfather, how can you?" Kate said reproachfully. She went to him and reaching him, she brushed back a stray wisp of his white hair. "Stop now—there's a dear! Do what Sir Richard says. Breathe—that's right—once again . . . now—tell us who's lost?"

"His car's—still here—he's gone," Wells gasped.

"Whose car?"

"The American."

The young men exchanged looks. "Is the car a dark green?" one of them inquired.

"It is," Wells said.

The young man turned to his comrades. "It's him."

"Think of him getting here like that, ahead of the train! And over these winding roads."

"He drives like crazy, if he doesn't see a cathedral."

Sir Richard held up his hand for silence. Instinctively they obeyed. "Do you mean to say," he inquired slowly, "do you mean to say that the—the fellow who arrived here ahead of the lot of you is Mr. John P. Blayne?"

"Who else?" one of the young men replied.

"But he's lost," Lady Mary put in.

"Nonsense," Sir Richard said with decision. "We must find him. We'll all scatter. At the end of half an hour we'll meet in the great hall and compare notes if we haven't found him."

"But what does he look like?" Kate demanded.

"Like nobody I have ever seen before," Wells groaned.

"Oh, come now," a young man objected. "He's a typical American—tall, brown hair, blue eyes—"

"Brown eyes," a second young man said.

"Well, eyes, anyway—wearing a gray suit—wasn't it

gray, fellows? No? Well, anyway a suit. Probably a red tie."

"And I told him to stay at the service door," Wells moaned. " 'Can't I get out and look about a bit?' he asks. 'No!' I tell him. 'You stay where you are, *if* you please, young chap, until I get my orders!' When I went back, he'd gone, clean as a whistle. I shouted for him and heard nothing but the bird in the big oak tree that mocks me when I call the kitchen cat."

Kate turned to Sir Richard with an air of petty authority. "Sir Richard, dear, you and Lady Mary must go and sit down in the hall and wait for us. Grandfather, you make them a cup of tea and drink one yourself in the pantry. The rest of us—" her dark eyes swept over the four young men—"the rest of us will find him. And mind you don't trample the flower beds, you young chaps, and don't break the yew branches to look through. The great hall's inside the great door here when you return, and stay there, if you please. Don't go wandering about inside the castle until I come back."

"Yes, ma'am," a young man said.

"Yes, *ma'am*—yes, ma'am—just as you say, ma'am."

They filed away making great pretense of obedience and Wells turned unsteadily and disappeared into the great door.

Lady Mary went to Kate and touched her cheek with a light kiss. "Thank you, my dear!"

"Ah, what would we do without you?" Sir Richard muttered. His head was pounding again in beats of pain.

"Come with me, my dears," Kate said in her richly comforting voice.

She stepped between them, and with an arm of each she led them toward the hall, talking all the while.

"I'm very cross, you know—this American, how dare he make such a disturbance? I asked the other chaps why he hadn't come on the train with them properly as he said he would and they just shrugged their shoulders."

She shrugged her shoulders elaborately to illustrate, glancing up to Sir Richard on her right then to Lady Mary on her left. They were not smiling as she meant them to, so she went on with determined cheerfulness.

"The stories they told me about him! He drives a motor like a devil, won't have a chauffeur, they said—but he'll stop for hours in some old cathedral and they don't know where he is." Kate tossed her head. "And to think that I got up an hour earlier than I needed to this morning to have the castle looking nice! All that cleaning and dusting, though why I want to make a good impression on him when it's to sell the castle—" Suddenly she had lost her tone of gay defiance. "Oh dear, oh dear, I do love this old place!" she said wistfully.

They were in the great hall now. She walked them straight through it into their own sitting room beyond and there she settled them in their chairs. Once she could get behind their backs she wiped her eyes hastily with her handkerchief and tidied the books on the table as she talked.

"I can't bear for strangers to see the castle except when it's at its best—it's what he is, that American, only a stranger—and I wish he'd stayed at home. Ah well, I shan't hurry myself for him anymore, wherever he's wandering."

"Stop worrying yourself, Kate," Lady Mary said mildly, "and tell Wells to bring us some tea. I feel quite faint."

"He'll bring it, my lady, and if you'll excuse me, I will go about the grounds and see that the men aren't tearing everything to bits."

She left them, stopping in the hall to look at herself in the mirror, for after all she'd been through she had no doubt that she wanted tidying herself. The image in the mirror was on the whole satisfactory however, her cheeks pink from being angry and her hair curling with the damp morning air. Feeling better after what she saw, she went out into the grounds again, down the gravel walk toward the yews.

He'd be there, perhaps, for they were famous, those great yews carved and trimmed in the shape of marching elephants. She looked down the long vista, the gigantic shrubs towering above her head, but no one was there. . . . He'd be in the rose garden, maybe, and thither she went but he was not there nor in the spinney beyond the kitchen gardens and the henhouses. She decided to go to the lake and see if he might be wandering in the forest beyond, calculating on the value of the trees and adding up his profits for cutting them down. That indeed she felt she could not bear, for the oaks were huge and worth a fortune, only not enough, Sir Richard had often said, to save the situation.

Suddenly she saw him. He was walking toward the lake, not from the wood, but down the slope of the lawn. Yes, it could be none but the American, a tall, lean man in a dark gray suit, but much younger than she had thought he would be. His step was easy and carefree as though he already owned the land upon which he walked. Sure of himself, was he? Kate asked herself as she followed him silently, staying near enough to a tree here and there so that she could slip behind it if he turned. She'd follow and see what he did and where he went when he thought nobody was watching him.

To her surprise, he went nowhere. He stood at the lake's edge for minutes and then sat himself down on the grass comfortably as though he meant to spend the day. He was staring at something in the lake but what? Suddenly he threw back his head and gave a shout of laughter. She was mystified. Why was he laughing all by himself? Drunk, maybe, perhaps not quite right in the head? She tiptoed over the grass until she stood almost behind him. He was actually talking to himself!

"That's it, fella! Be careful now—you'll choke—a spider is a mean thing to swallow!"

No—yes! He was talking to a frog! There on a lily pad a huge green bullfrog sat in the sun, its red thread of a tongue flicking in and out.

"Whatever are you doing?" she asked severely.

He gave a start and leaped to his feet.

"Trespassing, that's what," she went on, looking him over from head to foot. He was even taller than she thought and she tilted her head at an absurd angle to meet his eyes—blue eyes, they were, but on the gray side; he had a good mouth, it was firm and yet—pleasant was the word.

He was the American, of course, and she could have wished he weren't so handsome. He had a nice smile, too —shy and friendly at the same time and good white teeth showing through it.

"I'm sorry," he said. "Though I am here on business of a sort, so perhaps you'll forgive me."

She tried to look prim. "It's not for me to forgive or not. The castle belongs to Sir Richard and Lady Mary."

"I hope the frog goes with the castle. He has such a proprietary air."

He was making jokes, was he? Well, she would get back at him by pretending she didn't know who he was, though there was no mistaking him with that dark gray suit and red tie.

"If you've come to sell something," she said unsmiling, "then take yourself off. We never buy anything here at the castle. Just keep straight up the path and you'll come to the gate and beyond that the highway direct to London." She walked away and stopped. She'd been a bit too harsh, perhaps? "You may have the frog if you like," she called to him over her shoulder. "I hate frogs," she added.

He was after her at once. "May I come with you? I've lost my way, I'm afraid, and I left my car somewhere."

She had to down him. "You shouldn't have come into the grounds without permission."

"Well, you see—"

"I don't see! I still say it's trespassing!"

They faced each other, eyes gazing into eyes.

"I'm sorry," he said and turned away.

She let him walk twenty yards or so and then she called again. Oh, she could be wicked, too, a cat playing with a mouse! "Did you happen by any chance to see an old man wandering about? We've lost him."

He walked halfway back. "Lost him?"

"Yes."

"How does he look?"

"I've never seen him to know who he was."

"Then how can you say you've lost him?"

"Not I, exactly! He came to see Sir Richard—about the castle. We're rather glad he's lost."

"Glad?"

"Yes, but I suppose he must be found." She walked toward him. "Come along—you may as well join in the search now that you're here. He's a sort of monster, you know."

"Monster?"

"Yes, with money," and in the way she said "money" was all her passionate defense of the castle.

They were walking side by side. Accidentally, of course, she was not looking at him, but he stealing looks at her; she continued absently, as if it did not matter what she said to a transient, a wanderer, who had no business here and could not be concerned.

"He wants to buy the castle."

"Really?"

"Yes, for a museum. We love the castle and we loathe him."

"Then why do you sell the castle?"

"It's not mine. It belongs to the family. But I've lived here all my life. My father was born here. So was my grandfather."

She stopped and sighed. "But why should we bother to find him? I've looked everywhere. Perhaps he's gone away. I hope he has. And I'll take you to the service entrance."

"Thank you."

They walked in silence for a moment until she saw the car. Yes, it was a green car.

"This is your motorcar?"

"Yes."

"Nice—"

She looked at it carelessly and turned away. "Well—good-bye. "

"Would you—"

"Yes?"

"I shouldn't ask but—now that I'm here—"

"What?"

"I do want to see the inside of the castle. I've heard about it. An ancient man was here but he couldn't let me go in."

"That was my grandfather."

"You don't look a bit like him!"

"How could I?"

"Then will you—"

He smiled at her and she tried not to smile back. "Will you go away at once if I let you see the castle?"

"If you want me to—"

"I won't take you to the part where the family lives, you know."

"Of course not."

"Very well, then—but only for a bit."

With elaborate deceit she began the tour she knew so well. There was no one in the kitchens, no one in the pantry. She led him up a small winding staircase to a narrow passage, and then up still another staircase to small old rooms above, talking as she went.

"This is the original part of the castle. Queen Elizabeth was the one who built it bigger. Shakespeare was here, they say, and here he showed the Queen his *Midsummer Night's Dream*. And quite recently, Charles Dickens was here."

"Recently?"

"Only a century ago—that's nothing—"

"How does this part connect with the rest?"

"There's a passage here. Be careful! That's a trapdoor."

She drew him aside hastily. He looked down and saw at his feet a heavy iron ring in a rotting floor.

"Trapdoors everywhere," she explained. "They lead straight down to the dungeons."

"Dungeons?"

"The castle was a royal seat for five hundred years, and kings and queens are always putting people in dungeons, it seems—or used to. You could have fallen for miles, you know."

"Not really miles?"

"I daresay you would think it miles if you were falling."

They laughed together unexpectedly and something warm was in the laughter. Now it was she who stumbled suddenly on a warped board and he caught her.

"Careful there—"

She drew away from him. "I'm quite all right, thank you. I know the castle, probably better than anyone. I used to explore it as a child."

"Weren't you ever frightened?"

"Not really—I felt safe here. I was accustomed to being alone. And they were always kind to me."

"They?"

"Sir Richard and Lady Mary."

Why was she telling him all this? Like as not he was laughing at her. She glanced at him and saw no difference in the smiling eyes. But the joke was ended for her. She put out her hand frankly.

"Of course I know who you are, Mr. Blayne. I can't think why I've been—mischievous!"

His mouth twitched—ah, it was a good mouth, sensitive and warm.

"I haven't been quite honest, either, I'm afraid," he said.

"But you couldn't know me," she exclaimed.

"No, but I've had a hunch—"

"Hunch?"

"An idea—a conviction—all along, that you knew who I was and why I was here."

"Oh—"

"So now that we've both confessed and are honest again, will you tell me who you really are?"

She looked him straight in the eyes. "I'm Kate."

"Kate? Kate who?"

"Kate Wells, the maid."

"Miss Kate Wells," he said slowly, looking down into her flushed face.

"Just Kate." She drew back and then stepped ahead of him. "This way, please, Mr. Blayne. They are waiting for you in the great hall."

She went ahead of him through passages so narrow that there was no possibility of their walking side by side until she came to the small door which led into the great hall. There she was delayed for a moment because the latch was rusty and would not turn. He caught up with her.

"Please—"

She refused to yield. "You don't know the latch as well as I do. It'll give in a minute."

He waited for the minute and then took her by the shoulders and set her firmly aside. She caught her breath in surprise and said nothing. Let him! He wouldn't be able to move the latch, but he'd have to find out for himself, cocksure as he was. To her chagrin the willful latch yielded at once and the door swung open. Inside the hall the four young men, who had long since given up their search, were sitting in the carved oaken chairs. At sight of him they made cries more of welcome than surprise.

"Here's John Preston Blayne at last!"

"And we thought you were lost!"

Kate broke across their exclamations. "I don't think you've been looking for him at all."

The youngest one grinned clean across his face. "We didn't need to, did we? He always turns up, and in the best of company."

John Blayne laughed.

"We've brought the blueprints and are ready to get to work, John, just as soon as you say the word." To prove it, the young man unrolled a set of papers he had been holding and spread them out flat on the table.

"Work!" Kate exclaimed. "Whatever do they mean?" Startled, she looked from the sheets of blue paper to Mr. Blayne, then to each of the four young men in turn, all of them looking so out of place in the great hall of the castle.

"Lay off, fellows," John Blayne said good-naturedly. "I don't blame Miss Wells for being shocked. You're premature. Things aren't settled yet, not by a long shot. Fold up your tents now and steal away until tomorrow. You have rooms at the village inn."

Levity was blown away like mist before a gale. In spite of his casual air, John Blayne's voice held authority. The young men looked at one another. The eldest coughed and cleared his throat. "As a matter of fact, John, it's lucky you turned up at this moment. I'm glad nothing is settled. The job is impossible."

John Blayne looked from one of his men to another and Kate saw his face harden. Tough, was he? Or just used to getting his own way?"

"Impossible?" he said quietly. "I don't recognize the word."

"The beams are too weak," one young man urged.

Kate burst into the argument. "Weak, are they? You'd be weak, if you'd been put up a thousand years ago. Weak! They're as solid as the Bank of England."

John Blayne threw her a look, amused again and gay. "Thank you, Miss Wells. And you, fellows—I know the castle isn't Buckingham or Windsor, it's too old. That's the beauty of it, and that's why we must take it down, stone by stone—"

They went into chorus again. "Part of it is brick"— "Those bricks will crumble to dust"—"We're lucky if we can transport half of them."

He cut them short. "You underestimate English workmanship!"

The argument grew hot. The nameless young men— and Kate was sure they were nameless because they looked so much alike, with their short noses and strong chins and similar haircuts—rushed into the deepening fray.

"You've done a lot of crazy things, John, but this is the craziest."

"Remember that Japanese temple you bought and took to New York? Still lying in the warehouse—even the Met wouldn't have it—nobody dares to tackle putting it together again. Why don't you use that for a museum?"

"And that painting you said had to be restored—"

John Blayne stood rock firm, smiling, enjoying the onslaught, waiting until they were out of breath.

"Now," he said. "Have you got everything off your chests? Yes, I'm crazy—but I get what I want in the end, remember that! Why don't I put up the Japanese temple? Some day, at the right time in the right place, I will, and I'll dare you chaps to tackle the job and you'll take the dare. I don't want a temple for a museum, the ghosts of Buddhist monks meditating among fat Rubens women and Roman gods and goddesses! A castle is exactly what I want and exactly what I'll have. And I was right about the painting, wasn't I? Under that hodgepodge of oils there was a Raphael. I could smell it. I shall hang it right there, above the chimney piece."

Grim silence fell. The eldest young man sighed and took a notebook and pencil from his pocket. "All right, but it will cost a small fortune—every brick to be wrapped in tissue paper—"

"Remind me to order a hundred tons of tissue paper."

"And ships to transport the bricks and stone—"

"Remind me to order ten ships instead of the two we have."

The young man turned to his fellows and shrugged, his eyebrows arched in dismay.

"All right, men, let's take his dare and tear down the castle!"

Kate could bear no more. She stood listening to the arguments in progressive horror. She looked now at the blueprints outspread upon the table and saw the castle standing not on this green English hill, but in a rugged landscape somewhere far away, and surrounded not by English meadows and by calm brooks, but by wooded mountains and a rocky seacoast. Comprehension flashed upon her mind.

"You're not—you're not going to take the castle to America? But that's insane, Mr. Blayne! It can't be done, besides Sir Richard won't allow it. I'm sure he thought the museum was to be here! Wait—I'll fetch him and Lady Mary. No—no—they'll never be able to bear the shock. Oh, how to tell them . . ."

She hesitated and wrung her hands. The door behind her opened. Wells looked in and turned to announce what he saw.

"The gentleman's been found, Sir Richard, and my lady!"

They were there before she could speak, the two of them coming in together, bravely smiling. Sir Richard put out his hand.

"How do you do, Mr. Blayne? You gave us quite a start, not knowing who you were exactly nor where you'd gone. It's shockingly easy to be lost in the grounds hereabout. I'm sorry—do forgive us!"

John Blayne accepted the hearty handshake and controlled his instinctive wince. What a grip these old Englishmen had! "My fault entirely, Sir Richard. I shouldn't have been so unceremonious in my arrival."

He turned to Lady Mary. "My apologies to you, too, Lady Mary."

She was pink with effort, Kate observed. Ah, the sweet darling, trying so hard not to mind! Kate glanced at Mr. Blayne, then looked quickly away. She would not help him one bit in his predicament. Let him struggle his way through the mess he'd made, not telling the truth to poor Sir Richard, who'd never have consented had he known —but Lady Mary was talking in her high fluting voice, her public voice, with which she opened bazaars and spoke at charity teas.

"Mr. Blade—"

"Blayne, my dear," Sir Richard put in.

"Ah yes—I'm sorry—American names are so difficult! I do assure you, now that we're used to the idea, we're almost quite reconciled, you know—it's a rather lovely idea to think of treasures of art hanging on our old walls—I daresay from our little nook in the gatehouse we'll come here often, as tourists, you know, and all that—Shan't we, Kate?"

She turned to Kate, but that stubborn young woman, her eyes brimming with tears, merely nodded. Lady Mary, seeing the tears, stared at her in amazement.

"Kate, whatever's wrong with you? Look, Richard, Kate's crying!"

"I'm not crying," Kate said passionately. "It's just that I'm trying not to—to—to—sneeze."

She turned her back and made a fine mock sneeze.

Lady Mary appealed prettily to John Blayne. "Oh dear, these old castles are damp, you know, Mr. Blayne. I hope you'll be prepared. I hope you aren't thinking of central heating and all that—bad for paintings, I'm sure. We've never considered it for ourselves, in spite of being quite miserably cold sometimes, especially if it's a gray winter without proper sun."

"You are very kind, Lady Mary," he said gently. He glanced at Kate's back.

"So surprising for an American," Sir Richard was saying, "this love of the past and your wanting an old castle—"

John Blayne glanced about the hall. He was facing his predicament alone. The four young men had taken his suggestion and removed themselves and the blueprints to the village inn. Kate stood at a window, her back obdurate. He rushed into hasty speech.

"Surprising, perhaps, Sir Richard, but I inherit my love of art from my mother. She loved old paintings and my father bought them for her—as an indulgence, I'm afraid. He hasn't the same taste. As it is, they've turned out to be his best investment now. I say now, because when my mother began collecting pictures before she died, about fifteen years ago, and it was apparent that I was to be the only child—which has nothing to do with anything, exactly, except that she wanted something to take up her mind when I was sent to Groton—my father thought it was an absurd obsession. But she went ahead and became really a connoisseur of twelfth- and thirteenth-century art which she afterwards extended to include as late as the seventeenth, particularly English."

"Interesting," said Sir Richard.

"My father adored her, and let her have her way. But when she died and her estate was assessed he was amazed—not to say floored—when our lawyers told him the collection was a very fine one, worth something over a hundred million dollars, and likely to triple that amount in his lifetime. He decided immediately that he would build a vaultlike sort of place in which to store the collection, a sort of private Fort Knox."

"Very interesting," said Sir Richard.

"But that seemed to me to be nothing short of a crime, because paintings are meant to be seen, you know, and so I protested. I must confess I could never have won against my father, if our lawyers had not had the bright idea of a Foundation."

"But, surely," Lady Mary observed, "the building would have had a foundation in any case."

John Blayne stared, then smiled. "No, no, Lady Mary —a 'foundation' in America means a fund set aside for a non-profit purpose, a public service of some sort. As our lawyers have pointed out to my father, if he builds a museum which would be open to the public, he will be able to finance it from this Foundation, which would be tax-deductible."

Lady Mary turned to Sir Richard. "Do you understand what he's saying?"

"Not yet, my dear," Sir Richard replied. "But I daresay I shall, in time."

"Do stay for luncheon with us so we can go on talking, Mr. . . ." Lady Mary paused.

"Blayne," Sir Richard supplied.

"I'd be delighted," John Blayne said, smiling down at the pair of them. "I wonder if you know how perfect you are in this setting—it's a way you English have, I think, of looking as though you've built your backgrounds to suit."

"They've built us, I fear," Sir Richard said, returning the smile but dimly.

Kate could bear no more. She turned on them in a fury. "Lady Mary, my dear, and Sir Richard, I assure you, neither of you has the faintest idea—I hadn't myself until—"

John Blayne threw her a desperate glance. "Miss Wells, please, I beg you. We have a lot to talk about of course, and I—"

"You're very right," Kate said hotly, "but it had better be said now. Sir Richard, I think you should know you and my lady—"

John Blayne was suddenly as angry as she. "Really, Miss Wells, this is entirely between Sir Richard and me. I don't see why you—Sir Richard, there has been a misunderstanding, which certainly can be set straight. On second thought, I'm not sure it is even a misunderstanding—perhaps only on the part of Miss Wells. Of course, she has not seen our correspondence."

"They'd have told me," Kate put in.

"Kate dear," Lady Mary said, wondering. "I can't think why you keep interrupting Mr. Blade."

"Blayne, my dear," Sir Richard said, but was ignored.

"It's he who is interrupting me, my lady," Kate said with passion.

"I think," Sir Richard suggested judiciously, "that we'd better let them have turns, my dear. Shall we say ladies first, Mr. Blayne? Or Kate, shall we give him the courtesy as our guest?"

They faced one another, John Blayne and Kate, neither willing to yield, both knowing that yielding there must be.

"Come, come," Sir Richard said gently.

John Blayne shrugged his shoulders. "I yield, Sir Richard—as an American, I'm trained to chivalry. Ladies first."

Sir Richard laughed. He was enjoying the contest. "Very nicely put, I must say! Did you hear that, my dear? Trained to chivalry he says—very nice, for an American, eh?"

Lady Mary met smile with smile. "He's much better than expected."

"Thank you," John Blayne said. "And now, if I may confess it, I'm delighted to accept your invitation to luncheon, Lady Mary."

She inclined her head and nodded to Wells. "Lay another place, Wells, and use the silver soup tureen." She glanced at the waiting men. "And in the small dining hall, just the three of us."

"Very good, my lady." Wells disappeared.

Through all this, Kate had waited in stiff patience. Lady Mary, it seemed, had forgotten the controversy and perhaps Sir Richard wanted it forgotten. Well, she insisted upon it. She turned to face them and spoke with firmness. "Mr. Blayne, pray proceed."

He answered with a sort of desperate gaiety.

"You have the floor, I believe, Miss Wells. No? Very well, then. Sir Richard, she's right—I'm planning a great piece of folly—quite terrible, in fact. I do plan to take it away."

Kate ignored the gaiety. "Sir Richard, it's the castle he's taking away."

Silence fell. Lady Mary broke it faintly. "Did you say *away*, Kate?"

"To America, my lady."

"To America?" Lady Mary echoed in a whisper. Then the monstrous meaning crept into her understanding. "Richard—he's taking the castle to America!"

Sir Richard went white, then the red came flashing up from his neck. He was suddenly half blind with pain stabbing at his temples. "Mr. Blayne, I don't understand."

"I can't blame you, Sir Richard," John Blayne said gently. "It's my fault. We should have had our lawyers handle the transaction—I'm always too informal—too impetuous—but I thought my letter would explain everything—would be enough . . ."

He reached into his pocket for a piece of paper which he unfolded and laid on the table. "Here's what I had in mind." It was a sketch of the castle, not in English meadows but against wooded hills.

Lady Mary fumbled for her spectacles, put them on and stared at the few words in the lower left corner. "Conn-Conn-"

"Connecticut," he said.

"What an odd name," she observed. "Is it the name of the artist?"

Sir Richard looked at it with detached interest. Nothing could matter until this hammer in his head ceased to pound. He forced himself to speak.

"Rather a nice drawing, my dear. It looks like the castle right enough—though the east tower is too short. The two towers should be the same height, Mr. Blayne."

Kate stepped forward, she put her hand on John Blayne's arm and spoke softly. "They still don't comprehend—they simply can't. You must help them—indeed you must."

He looked down at the small hand on his arm and then into her earnest eyes. He nodded, and she let her hand slip to her side.

"Sir Richard," he said, "let me remind you." He took a letter from his breast pocket and unfolded it. "I brought a copy of my letter to you, luckily. Perhaps you will recall—and Lady Mary, Connecticut is the name of a state, not of an artist. Let me read just this paragraph, Sir Richard. 'I intend to use this castle as the most beautiful museum ever conceived in Connecticut. The cost will be immense, but I am prepared to spend any amount in order that my mother's priceless collection of art can be properly housed for the public to enjoy.' . . . Doesn't this mean Connecticut, USA? I don't know of any other."

They were stricken, he could see that. Sir Richard sat down in a huge oak armchair. "I thought—*conceived* in Connecticut—I supposed it meant merely that you were speaking of the—the idea, you know."

"It's an invasion—that's what it is," Lady Mary cried, her soft voice suddenly shrill. "It's the Spanish Armada all over again, Richard."

Very straight and dignified, Sir Richard put up his hand for silence. He sat motionless, attentive only to the thunder in his skull. His gaze was fixed on some point in the distant end of the great hall and when at last he spoke it was as if he spoke to someone there, his voice low and unsteady. "I inherited Starborough Castle and the estate entire, including one thousand acres of forest and three thousand acres of farmlands, from my ancestors. It has belonged to my family for five hundred years. It was given to my ancestor, William Sedgeley, for extraordinary bravery in defending the King during a plot to assassinate. In each generation we have . . . done our best to care for castle and farm and forest. In my time, unfortunately, the world has changed so that a heritage such as mine has become an intolerable burden, far beyond the power of one man to bear. I am responsible for seventy families who live and work upon my land. . . . I . . . I . . ."

His voice failed. Kate ran to his side, Lady Mary sat down suddenly in a high-back chair. Her delicate face was white.

"Oh, my God," she murmured.

John Blayne went to her side but she pushed his hand away.

"Please," she murmured.

Kate looked earnestly at the American. "Mr. Blayne, I know what to do for them both, may I ask you to do something for me?"

"Yes indeed, Miss Wells, anything, anything at all. I had not intended to cause them such distress. I am sorry, believe me."

"Then"—she managed to smile in spite of her own inner heaviness—"will you join your men at the inn and come back instead for dinner? It will give Sir Richard and Lady Mary a little time to accustom themselves to— to this strange situation."

"Gladly, Miss Wells, but perhaps it would be better if I did not return until tomorrow?"

"Come back this evening," Sir Richard said in an unexpectedly firm tone. "We have not done talking, nor shall we until we understand each other."

Lady Mary lifted her head, proudly now, and as the lady of the castle she spoke. "And, of course, you will spend the night, Mr. Blayne."

"You're very kind, Lady Mary, but I don't want to put you to all that trouble. I shall get a room at the inn."

Wells, who had entered the room to announce luncheon, stood unobtrusively in the doorway. "Pardon me, my lady, but I understood that the gentleman from America was to stay at the castle. I have already removed his suitcase from his motorcar and unpacked it."

"Thank you, Wells. What room have you put him in?"

"The Duke's room, my lady."

"Take him to King John's room," Sir Richard said sternly.

"*Not* King John's room, Richard," Lady Mary replied in a low voice, looking earnestly at her husband. "The damp, you know, and besides *they've* been very noisy in that room lately. Haven't *they, Kate?*"

But Kate, engaged in another conversation, did not hear the question.

"I believe *they've* been taking heed of what's been going on. *They're* always ahead of us in these matters, you know."

Sir Richard smiled indulgently at his wife and the strain that had come over them both was momentarily eased. He turned to Wells. "The Duke's room it shall be, Wells."

"Very good, my lord."

While they were settling the matter of the room, Kate and John Blayne had been settling the matter of his return to the castle.

". . . yes, dinner is at eight, here in the great hall, and, *please,* Mr. Blayne, black tie."

"Oh, but of course!" He smiled his understanding of all she had been saying, nodded briskly to Sir Richard and Lady Mary, then walked toward the door that led out to the garden. He would not let himself look back, even before he went out the door. He felt that he could not bear it if Kate had turned away.

Only after the door closed behind him did Kate direct herself to her two charges. "And now, my two dears," she said with a lightness she had not thought she could muster, "won't you go in to your luncheon?"

Promptly at eight o'clock they sat down to dinner— Lady Mary and Sir Richard at either end of the long narrow table, John Blayne between them and on Lady Mary's right. Wells stood by the buffet, ready to serve. Kate, in black dress, small white apron and neat little cap perched on her brown curls, stood behind Lady Mary's chair. To John Blayne she looked like an actress, oddly charming in the part she now had to play; to the master and mistress of the castle she was only doing what she had done since she had been old enough to take her place in service.

As if a truce had been called, the conversation at dinner ranged from art to politics, from medieval history to contemporary drama, from the status of farming on both sides of the Atlantic to the importance of blood lines in breeding stock. The small roast was delicious, the wine was vintage; the dessert fruit was damsons bottled the previous summer from an ancient tree in the kitchen garden. The cheese was Stilton.

Only over their coffee cups in the small sitting room off the great hall was mention made of the business at hand. Kate had brought in the coffee tray and set it on a low table before Lady Mary. The American noticed that there were four cups on the tray and that Kate had left cap and apron in the kitchen.

"Black or white, Mr. Blayne?" Lady Mary asked as she poured.

"Black, please, Lady Mary."

The two men stood with their backs to the fire. Kate stood beside Lady Mary on a low couch.

"Tomorrow morning, Mr. Blayne," Sir Richard said casually, "I have asked my solicitor, Philip Webster, to join us for our discussion of this matter of the castle."

"I shall be happy to meet him."

"It is possible," Sir Richard hesitated, "that you might have liked to have your legal representative present, too. But I daresay you could not get him over from America in time for our meeting tomorrow." Sir Richard chuckled slightly.

"My lawyer, David Holt, of the New York firm of Haynes, Holt, Bagley and Spence, accompanied me to England, Sir Richard. He has been staying in London, but I made a telephone call to him this afternoon. He was due to arrive at the inn in the village this evening."

"Then we shall both have our advisers. Capital!" Sir Richard exclaimed. "Capital, indeed. Ten o'clock tomorrow morning in the great hall. Perhaps you would like to have a ride before breakfast? Wells could find you something to wear. My horse is spirited, but quite reliable. However, you might prefer her ladyship's, an older mount but strong in wind and limb."

"Thanks, Sir Richard, I should enjoy nothing more than an early-morning ride." He turned to Kate. "Would you join me, Miss Wells, and show me something of the countryside?"

She smiled up at him like a radiantly happy child, then shook her head. "I have duties in the morning, Mr. Blayne."

"I understand," he said quietly, then he turned back to Sir Richard. "Perhaps it would be well for me to retire now, Sir Richard, with all that is before us tomorrow."

"Quite so." Sir Richard moved toward a bell pull on the wall and the sound of a distant ringing could be heard. When Wells appeared in the doorway, Sir Richard spoke. "Take Mr. Blayne to the Duke's room, Wells."

"Yes, my lord."

"I'd better just go along with them and see that everything is right," Kate said. She took the coffee tray and went toward the door.

"How kind you are," John Blayne murmured.

He said good night and was halfway across the room when Lady Mary remarked, "Oh, I hope *they* won't bother you tonight."

"Careful, my dear. You must not mystify or frighten our guest out of his night's sleep."

"Don't worry about me, Sir Richard, I'm a good sleeper. I assure you, Lady Mary, that I shall be quite all right. Until the morning, then!" He stood in the doorway and lifted his hand in a gesture of farewell.

Sir Richard and Lady Mary were sitting together now

on the low couch. They looked regal, and yet tender at the same time, and thoroughly in command while the truce held. Swords would be drawn in earnest in the morning.

After the door had closed, Lady Mary sighed and laid her hand lightly on her husband's. "He's rather nice, Richard, don't you think, in spite of his being an—"

"Very nice," Sir Richard agreed, "surprising, as a matter of fact. One never knows Americans."

Wells opened the door to the Duke's room. "Here you are, sir. I hope you'll find everything to your satisfaction."

The bed had been turned down and John Blayne saw that his pajamas and robe had been laid on the faded coverlet; his slippers were neatly arranged on the floor. The light on the table by the bed gave a warmth which the room had lacked when he had gone to it before dinner to dress; a small fire in the grate had done its best to counteract the dampness.

"The candle, sir, is near the lamp, and there's a box of matches."

"Whatever do I need a candle for?"

"The electricity has a way of failing, sir, and some of the passages have no light in any case."

"But, Wells, I really don't expect to go wandering around the castle during the night."

"Very good, sir, but then you never know. Best be prepared is what I always say. If that is all, sir, I'll wish you a very good night."

"Thank you, Wells."

The old man turned and left. Kate busied herself about the room, testing the windowsills with her forefinger for dust, arranging the long satin curtains. It was an immense room, and the windows reached from floor to ceiling. The crimson satin curtains were shredding and she was trying to hide the rents. She caught his glance and dropped the curtain.

"You've a cut on your forehead," she said sharply and came to him to inspect.

He put his hand to his head. "I gave myself a blow this morning on that low door when we were going into the great hall."

"And you never said a word!" she cried.

"So much began to happen all at once."

"I must wash it immediately."

She went to a stand and poured water from a large porcelain pitcher into a basin and opened a drawer for a clean towel.

"It's nothing," he said.

"There's blood dried on it, under your hair," she retorted. "Stoop down, please—otherwise I'll have to fetch a step ladder."

He laughed and stooped down, and felt her light touch on his head as she washed the slight cut. A faint clean fragrance came from her. Her skin was very fine, her eyes more blue than any he had ever seen, a deep violet blue—very rare! One saw it in the paintings of the early madonnas. Her dark eyelashes were set thickly together and curled upward softly.

"You don't seem like an American," she was saying, as she kept at her self-appointed task. "Does that hurt?"

"Not in the least."

"Will you bend a little lower still, please? You're really shockingly tall, aren't you?"

"Depends on the girl I'm standing beside."

For the first time he heard her laughter, a lovely sound, free and warm.

"The inside of your mouth is pretty, too," he added.

She put her hand over her mouth. "I daresay you're looking straight down my throat—I forgot I was so close."

"I didn't."

She stepped back at that. "Now, really, Mr. Blayne—"

"Couldn't you call me John, as long as I'm in the castle?"

"I only know King John," she said, trying not to laugh.

"Ah, but he's dead!"

"I've started the bleeding, I'm afraid!" She came close again to wipe the blood away. "And King John isn't dead —altogether. He still has his room here—the one we didn't put you in. An old castle like this is always alive. At least it's—inhabited."

"Do you mean haunted?"

The lovely mouth was very near now, and he held himself taut. In the absorption in her task he saw her lips parted, the tip of her tongue between white teeth.

"No," she said, "not haunted. How can you be haunted by people you love? They are people—in different forms and shapes, perhaps, but alive."

She stepped back with a gesture encircling the room. "In this room, you may be wakened in the morning by bells from the royal chapel below. It's the ballroom now, but it was once the place where Queen Elizabeth knelt at dawn to pray. She prayed often—did you know that? People don't think of it, but she was religious. I daresay she was lonely and couldn't trust anyone—not even Essex whom she loved—perhaps especially Essex, because she'd told him she loved him, and so he had advantage."

"How do you know she told him?"

"She couldn't help it. Queen though she was, she fell in love like any woman. I daresay she fought her own heart, knowing she couldn't—mustn't—give herself into any man's power. But her heart won. It makes me glad I'm nobody."

"A beautiful little nobody!"

She laughed again. "I laid myself open, didn't I—but you needn't have taken notice!"

"I can't help noticing."

She pretended annoyance. "I shall have to stop talking altogether! There—it's only a scratch, after all." She walked away from him to the basin.

"No—no, please!" he said, following.

"If you keep teasing—" She was at the door now.

"Let's get back to the subject of the castle," he said. "Tell me more about it."

She considered, lingering on the threshold. "The reason I went with you in the passages is because they're quite dangerous, really—"

"Haunted, too?"

"No, but they lead to dungeons, I told you—and an underground river."

"Oh, come now—that's too perfect! It's what castles dream of having—dungeons and underground rivers."

"It's quite true. I could show you—"

"I want to be shown, I warn you!"

"And there's one window in the east tower that no one's ever been able to find the room to—"

"How do you know there's a room if no one's been able to find it?"

He was teasing again, but she was serious. She forgot herself, she walked toward him and came close, half whispering, her eyes enormous. "There was a big party here once, in King John's time, and they hung ribbons from every room, but there was one window with no ribbon to it—there's always been that one window!"

"Oh, come now!"

"It's true," she insisted. "There was a book in the library about the castle that told everything."

"I must see that book."

"Ah, it's been lost this long time—no one knows how. But my grandfather's seen it."

"If we take the castle apart, we'll discover its secrets."

"No—no, oh please, no! I don't want to know its secrets."

He was surprised to see her little face suddenly so troubled. "Tell me," he was serious now, "are the *they* that Lady Mary talks about part of the secrets?"

Kate did not look troubled now so much as she looked frightened. "That's not for me to say, Mr. Blayne." Then she had command of herself. Lifting her head, she gave him a formal little smile as though determined not to allow friendship. "I must get back to Lady Mary," she exclaimed. "She'll be wondering what's become of me."

She left him, standing alone in the Duke's room, and walked quickly along the winding stone-floored passage. In spite of her moment of panic, she felt inexplicably cheerful. She began singing under her breath. How wonderful life was, first frightening people to death and then making them feel that somehow things would be all right.

"Please do forgive me," she said, as she all but ran into the small sitting room.

"You've been a long time," Lady Mary remarked.

"It was the American, my lady. He asked ever so many questions about the castle."

"Questions, Kate, are to be answered tomorrow in the presence of our solicitors," Sir Richard reminded her gently.

"Yes, my lord."

"Now, go with her ladyship to her room. She should have been in bed an hour ago. It's been a wearying day."

"Yes, Sir Richard."

By ten o'clock the next morning they had gathered in the great hall, Sir Richard and Lady Mary, John Blayne and his lawyer David Holt, a smooth-shaven middle-aged man, slim and self-contained. Philip Webster was the last to arrive, but his presence was immediately felt. He was a short, stoutish man wearing no hat, a shaggy figure in wrinkled brown tweeds with a pipe in his mouth.

The moment he entered, Lady Mary turned to him and clasped her hands in piteous appeal. "Thank God, you've come, Philip."

Sir Richard turned to John Blayne. "My solicitor, Mr. Philip Webster of London. Webster, this is the—the American gentleman with whom you have had correspondence, I believe."

"And my lawyer, David Holt of Haynes, Holt, Bagley and Spence," John Blayne supplied.

Philip Webster removed his pipe, shook hands with John Blayne, and bowed without speaking to David Holt. Then he exploded to Sir Richard. "I say, Richard, what the devil is that gang of young men doing out by the gate? They drove in in a sort of shooting brake kind of thing just after I arrived. I asked them what they were about and they said they'd come to take measurements of the castle preparatory to removing it—as if it were a hen house or something!" He paused, then aware of the silence around him, exclaimed, "I say, what's wrong?"

Sir Richard did not reply for an instant. Pain had begun stabbing at his temples and he waited for it to abate. When he spoke, it was with his usual calm, but his manner was remote, as though he were not a part of what was taking place around him. "We're in a predicament, Philip, a sorry sort of business, and I don't quite see—I'm sure you didn't mean to deceive me, Philip, but the thing is very—" He looked at Lady Mary.

She was shaking her head.

"I'm afraid the sale can't go through, Philip, but what we shall do—"

"It's quite impossible," Lady Mary said. She was trembling slightly as she clasped her hands together. "But then, everything's impossible these days."

"*What* is impossible, Lady Mary?"

"They want to take the castle away and to a place I cannot even pronounce. Really, that's the most impossible thing I've ever heard of, and I shall never understand how you could think it possible. Philip, I simply cannot—"

"By Jove," Webster exclaimed, "the men were right then! But it's incredible. And, of course, I agreed to no such thing. How could I imagine anyone's taking the castle to America? What next! It's mad, quite, quite mad—"

John Blayne came forward, his hand outstretched and holding the letter.

"It's not mad, really. We're quite accustomed to moving large buildings to where we want them." With quiet precision he placed the letter flat on the table for anyone to read.

No one made a move to look at it. No one spoke.

"I'm very sorry for all this, Mr. Webster," John Blayne went on. "It's simply one of those misunderstandings that seem to arise between continents these days. Please read this. It's my letter. You should have had a copy, but I supposed that of course Sir Richard would have shown it to you."

Mr. Holt spoke. "I was afraid of this, Blayne. I distrust informality."

"Very dangerous," Webster added.

John Blayne gave him a quick glance, half impatient, half humorous. He was about to speak, but Mr. Holt prevented him by speaking first. "Mr. Webster is right, the situation calls for negotiation."

"Very dangerous otherwise," Philip Webster remarked, pleased that his point had been made.

John Blayne turned to Philip Webster and waited while the letter in question was carefully read.

"It's really not the sort of thing that ordinary individuals should undertake, you know," Webster said, pursing his lips and shaking his head. "Only lawyers should handle this sort of thing. Of course, my clients are quite right, too. It's impossible. We English don't export our castles, you know." He turned to Sir Richard. "There'll be litigation, I'm afraid. It may be very nasty. One never knows. But we'll have to go through with it."

Lady Mary, who had sat nervously twisting her fingers, rose with a sudden graceful movement from her chair. "I think at this moment, gentlemen, we could all do with a cup of tea." She went to the bell pull on the wall and jerked it vigorously. Down through distant corridors the jangling could be heard.

When Wells appeared, she asked him to send Kate with tea for them all. "We are five, Wells," she announced, as if she could not trust the old man's eyesight.

"Very good, my lady." He turned quickly and left the room. Aware of what the meeting was about, he was not willing to have them see the tears he could not control and that were already finding their way down his time-worn face.

During the interlude the two lawyers remained silent and watchful.

"There won't be any litigation," John Blayne said. "I certainly shan't force Sir Richard against his will. How-ever,—well, here's the check for the agreed sum—one million dollars, just to prove that I came in good faith."

There was a small gasp from Lady Mary. Kate, coming in with the tray of steaming teacups, looking up at John Blayne. Their eyes caught each other's for an instant of time.

"The letter is a commitment, Mr. Blayne." David Holt's words were measured. "And I must remind you also that you have already spent fifty thousand dollars, that you have engaged two ships, that you——"

Webster interrupted bluntly. "The letter wouldn't stand up in an English court of law, sir."

"We are Americans and deal in American law, sir," Holt retorted.

"My client is an Englishman, sir!" Webster rejoined.

"Being an Englishman doesn't excuse him from what a letter says in plain English," Mr. Holt declared, "especially since I have a letter in our files accepting our proposition."

"And I maintain he can't accept what he doesn't understand," Webster insisted.

The American lawyer persisted. "We have already brought over a group of architectural experts. Our technicians will soon follow. Vast plans have been made and contracts assigned. This was done following your letter of acceptance. The damages will be costly if everything must be canceled."

Webster dashed his pipe on the floor and ran his stubby hands through his reddish-gray hair until it stood in a curly tangle. "Try it, sir, just you try it! It'll be Agincourt again, I daresay, but remember who won! The castle's on English soil."

"Stop this!" The imperious voice was John Blayne's.

They stopped. Before their eyes he tore the check into small pieces and let the pieces flutter to the floor. Then he took the letter from the table, folded it into its envelope and handed it to Sir Richard.

"This is yours, Sir Richard. Do with it as you will. I didn't come here to bargain. I came with one simple purpose—to find a beautiful way to show great paintings by great artists. I wanted them to hang where people could see them—yes, my people—Americans—I wanted to share the paintings with them instead of having them locked away in a vault like so much gold bullion. I suppose you wonder why—"

"Please, gentlemen," interrupted Kate, "your tea!"

"Yes, yes," Lady Mary exclaimed, her voice shrill with

excitement. "Draw your chairs up to the table and let us partake of—of—"

"One of the most civilized of all pursuits," David Holt said gallantly, raising his cup toward her as he would have raised a glass of champagne in toast.

They drew their chairs up to the table. Kate moved around, offering them milk and sugar.

"Yes," Sir Richard said, stirring the sugar in his cup but looking at John Blayne, "I think you have made us wonder why."

John looked around the great hall—first at the tapestried walls, then at the faces of the people drawn up to the table. "Perhaps it's because I feel some sort of guilt, though I do not expect you to understand what I mean. My father is a wealthy man. His fortune was made in ways that—well, that seemed best to him. My mother was a different sort of person altogether . . ." He hesitated.

"A charming woman," David Holt said reminiscently.

"I think," John Blayne went on, "that I want to make a return of some sort for all that he . . ."

"Does your father know about this idea of yours?" Sir Richard asked.

"Of course, Sir Richard, and he thinks it sheer folly. But, to be quite honest with you, my father and I have rarely agreed on anything. We quarrel at least every other day."

"There!" Philip Webster spluttered.

"But, when I reminded him that since I was administering the Foundation—and he had asked me to, mind you —I must do things my own way."

"But why this way, pray?" Sir Richard demanded. "To spite your father, perhaps—because he wants to build something of his own?"

John Blayne got up from the table, walked away restlessly and as restlessly back again. "I don't want to spite

my father—I'm fond of him, and we both loved my
mother in our different ways. No, I want the castle
because it's the right idea. Great paintings can only live in
an harmonious atmosphere. Our museums are crowded.
I want my museum—well, harmonious. There's an old
Chinese saying—Lao-tse, I think. Someone asked him
if a certain task was being done properly and he said,
'The way is a way, but it is not the eternal way.' This
castle—it's stood in England for a thousand years. It'll
stand there in Connecticut for thousands more when we
are all dead—the paintings safe forever and living for
the joy of the generations we'll never see. Can you
understand how deeply I feel about buying something
as beautiful as this castle, this bit of England? I'm
English, myself, by ancestry."

Lady Mary nodded as if, against her will, she understood. Kate, too, nodded but the men remained grim-
faced.

"I remember how my mother bought the paintings.
She didn't know about art at first—she could only feel it.
Then as she grew to love it, she began to understand and
to know. One day she bought a Fra Angelico from an
old Italian in Venice—he was using it as a board to
display his fish. She didn't know it was valuable—only
that it was beautiful. She never did care about the money
value—that was one of those things my father couldn't
possibly understand. She told me—it was one of the last
things she ever said—'John, take care of my treasures.'
And I *will* take care of them, I want them to *be*—not
only for the sake of my mother, but for the sake of the
artists who created them. My mother understood those
artists—she knew what they wanted to say. She'd sit
hours before a painting, drinking it in. There's little
enough of that sort of pure love in the world today—
or of any sort, maybe. I shan't give up my idea, Sir

Richard! If I can't have this castle I'll find one some-where in England!"

He turned to Philip Webster. "Sorry, sir, the deal is off."

"I can't approve, John," Mr. Holt said.

John Blayne smiled. "I'll meet you at the inn before we go back to London."

David Holt nodded around the table, picked up his briefcase and quietly left the room. John made as if to follow, then paused, bit his lip and put out his hand to Webster. "Good-bye! You'd have put up a good fight—but there won't be a fight. You've won without it."

"I'm very happy if it is so, Mr. Blayne. You're a rarely generous opponent—rare, indeed."

"Not at all—not a fighter, perhaps. My father's the fighter. One's enough in a family, I daresay. But I won't have a beautiful plan spoiled by quarreling. Good-bye, Sir Richard—Lady Mary! You belong here, both of you. You're part of the castle and all it means to England—and to the rest of us in the world. . . . Miss Wells—"

He did not put out his hand for Kate and she noticed. Not for anything would she put out hers to him, then. She lifted her head and met his eyes straight. A glint of a smile came into his frank eyes. "Your frog will be safe, now. He can sit on his lily pad for the rest of his life."

He was loath to go, and he lingered, smiling at them with unconscious wistfulness. He liked them. They were people whom he could trust, people secure enough in themselves, even though they belonged to another age, not to fear wealth and its power. He was drawn to Sir Richard and Lady Mary with an affection which surprised him and warmed him. And Kate—he called her that to himself—she somehow belonged to these two in a way he did not yet understand, and he wanted to understand. She had a sturdy grace, a healthy beauty of her own. He could not explain her. Nor, for that matter, could he

explain his own curiosity. There was something appealing
in her smallness, perhaps, a delicacy that made her air
of self-reliance and competence amusing. She was an
unselfish little creature, her hair a tumble of natural
curls, and her face without makeup, a refreshing contrast
to the young women who populated his environment
somewhat too thickly. He felt that even his father might
agree with him about Kate if he could ever meet her;
agree with him, for once, and be willing to put Louise
aside.

Lady Mary rose from the table. "Surely we have not
finished talking?" She looked from one to the other
questioningly. "There must be a great deal more to be
said. We can do it over luncheon. Mr. Blade must be
starving."

Sir Richard rose to stand beside her. It was sweet,
John Blayne thought, watching them, how when one
took a stand the other came to the same spot. He would
always remember them, side by side in ancient splendor.
It was an achievement to grow old with splendor.

"If you will excuse me, Lady Mary, I think that I
must join my men and Mr. Holt at the inn. The shift of
events may have made them a little uncertain."

"But you will return for dinner? And surely you will
spend the night again?"

"Yes, indeed," Sir Richard added, "you must stay the
night, Mr. Blayne." Then he bent toward Lady Mary.
"Not *Blade,* my dear."

John Blayne hesitated and in the hesitation Wells entered.

"Your car, Mr. Blayne, shall I bring it around?"

"Yes, if you will, Wells, but—" He looked from one
to the other while avoiding even so much as a glance at
Kate. How far did he dare to allow himself the luxury of
enjoying this English warmth? It occurred to him, as he
stood in the vast old hall with the sunlight shining

through the high mullioned windows set deep in the thick stone walls, that it had been a long time; not since his mother died had he been aware of simple human warmth. "I will return," he said, smiling at them all.

Philip Webster enjoyed his luncheon as only a victor can. "Well, we won," he exclaimed for the third time, "and no one can say that it wasn't a dangerous situation. They could have sued us for breach of promise, Richard, though I'd have fought to the end for your sake."

Sir Richard turned on him, his heavy eyebrows bristling. "Are you telling me that I broke my word? I never break my word."

"No, no," Webster said hastily. "Good God, it'll never do to get you into a point of honor, Richard! There'd be no end to that. I'm only thinking of the future. What shall we do next? We're exactly where we were before all this began."

Lady Mary sighed. "A prison or an atomic plant— that's the choice, isn't it? It does seem a castle that's been the very root of England could be used for something in between, don't you think? But there's not to be any betweens nowadays, somehow. I can't think why. Isn't there someone you could telephone to in London, Philip? The Prime Minister or Chancellor of the Exchequer or someone—"

"I might try the National Trust again. One never knows when there'll be a change of heart," Webster suggested.

"By all means," Sir Richard said. "You should call them every day, twice, at least. Those fine arts chaps are always tea-drinking and forgetting what's practical."

"I'll try again," Webster said, "and I'll do it now."

He ambled out of the room.

Sir Richard looked after him gloomily. "I must tell

you, my dear, that I question whether Philip can handle the matter. I believe he quite regrets there being no lawsuit. It would have given him a chance to write endless papers no one could understand and brief barristers in front of everybody in the court, you know, and spout the stuff that lawyers can spew out on a moment's notice. They're all actors, in my opinion, and no more reliable when it comes to facts. They're always harking back to precedents that other lawyers have made for centuries past."

"I'm sure he could never find a precedent for selling a castle to— What's that place, Richard?"

"I can't pronounce it."

Lady Mary sighed. " 'Connect-i-cut,' I think? Fancy having one's castle moved to a place one can't pronounce!"

"Well, but Webster's right on one count, you know, my dear. Our difficulties are profound. You know the only private offers we've had in spite of all the advertising —a boys' school and an insane asylum. I simply won't mention the prison, or the atomic plant. They wouldn't use the castle for those, they'd raze it to the ground. All those scientist chaps want is empty space—a bit of a desert, as I told you. Our English scientists dream of equaling the Americans—those splendid deserts! Fancy a thousand acres of desert here in England!"

She heard this with horror, her fascinated eyes, still childishly blue, upon his face. "You could put in the bill of sale that they mustn't," she suggested. "You know you've always said that the castle wasn't to be changed. That's why that American millionaire from Hollywood wouldn't buy it. He said he'd put in central heating and American plumbing and you said—"

"Never mind, my dear. Americans always want to change things. At least there's this to be said for this Blayne chap—"

"John—"

"Ah, yes, yes—John, you know—he wants to put the castle up exactly as it is. Has he said anything about central heating?"

"No, he hasn't. Nor plumbing."

"As to plumbing, one wouldn't want bathers in a museum though Americans seem to want them everywhere. But the idea of moving the castle? I agree with his father, it would be sheer folly— *Why* doesn't he move Connecticut here?"

Kate entered the room with a bowl of tulips which she placed on the table. "Lovely, aren't they, my lady? And they've come so fast on the daffodils, as if everything about the castle wanted to look its best this spring."

"You sound quite pleased," Sir Richard said.

"And why not? You did manage well, Sir Richard dear! When the American saw how you felt about the castle, he knew he was honor bound to yield. He is honorable, don't you think?"

Only when she saw that her gaiety did not serve to cheer them did she realize their state of mind. They were sitting quietly, Lady Mary with her hands folded in her lap, and Sir Richard with his knees crossed. Their faces were grave, their eyes far away, looking as though they were not even listening to her.

"Whatever is the matter, my own dears?" she inquired tenderly.

She knelt impulsively before Lady Mary and chafed her narrow old hands, thin little hands, Kate always thought, like small plucked birds.

"We are very badly off, Kate," Sir Richard said. "Nothing is any better, really."

"How would you like to see the castle made into a prison?" Lady Mary asked mournfully.

"Ah, but it can't be that bad," Kate said. "You're just

tired, the two of you, and I can't blame you. I'm exhausted myself."

"I shall have to keep my word to this American," Sir Richard went on. "Even if I broke it—which I am not willing to do, mind you—I'd have to be talking to someone else in a week from now, and about something else."

She rose to go to him, but he would not be comforted.

"No, no, Kate," he groaned, pushing her away. "You don't understand. No one does. I must be by myself for a bit."

And he lifted himself out of the deep armchair and went from the room.

She returned then to Lady Mary, and drawing up a footstool, she sat down at her side. A dying fire burned under the chimney piece but in spite of it the room seemed chill.

"Is it really so desperate, my lady?" she asked.

"It is," Lady Mary said and sighed. "And what worries me most, Kate, is what *they* will say."

"I've thought of that, too."

Sometimes when they were alone, Kate leaned her head against Lady Mary's knee, as though she were a child again. She did so now and felt Lady Mary's hand smoothing her hair. She took the gentle hand and laid her cheek against it. "We've always respected *them*," Lady Mary went on. "We let *them* move about at night, even when it keeps us awake. And nothing can stop those bells! If we worry about *them* so much, one would think *they* could do a little worrying about us, now wouldn't one?"

"If *they* know," Kate said. "Yet how can *they* help us even if *they* do know? *They* may be far more helpless than we think, poor things! It's all a matter of waves, I sometimes fancy!"

"Waves?" Lady Mary repeated vaguely.

"Like the wireless, you know, my lady. No wire,

nothing one can see, but the voices come in. Only we don't have something in ourselves that we can turn on. Perhaps *they* try all sorts of ways to break through to us and can't."

Lady Mary seemed not to be listening. "If only *they* could help us to find a treasure hidden somewhere," she mused. "Of course Richard says it's nonsense because all castles are supposed to have treasures hidden in them by ancestors, but if it's always supposed to be so, perhaps sometimes it is so."

"Maybe King John would tell us, if I got up early when the bell rings."

She spoke half playfully and Lady Mary did not answer for a moment. When she did her voice was grave.

"Kate, are we mad, do you think?"

Kate kissed the hand she held. "Certainly not. Did you ever make anything up out of your head, my lady?"

"Never," Lady Mary said fervently. "Never, never! One of *them* always told me."

"Then *they* do get through sometimes and we must simply try our best to get help from *them*," Kate said.

She rose to mend the fire and put on a log. When she spoke again her voice was carefully indifferent. "Too bad the American came here with such a stupid idea! He's rather nice—and not at all stupid, really."

She broke off with a laugh. "That frog—so amusing!"

Lady Mary stared at her open-mouthed. She was about to inquire why the laughter and what about the frog, pray tell, but the look on Kate's face silenced her. What was happening? There was more than amusement in that look. There was tenderness.

. . . Sir Richard reined in his horse and gazed over his fields. A faint mist had all but obscured the sun since noon, but as the afternoon hours lengthened, the mist had burned away, and the sun shone full upon the enlivened landscape. It was a fair sight, the fields green with early corn and his good Guernsey cows grazing the rolling meadows. In the distance a cluster of roofs showed the village, and here and there a few trees sheltered a cottage for a farm family.

How eternal the landscape! Fields, meadows and forests were his by the divine right of ancient kings long dead, but who before they died had bequeathed this part of their realm to William Sedgeley, his ancestor. He was proud of the fact that he looked like William. Even as a boy his mother had said, "Richard looks so much like Sir William. I wish we'd named him William." The portrait of William hung over the chimney piece in the ballroom, a tall slim man on horseback, his head held high. There was royal blood somewhere in the Sedgeleys —hidden, of course. A rumor, spoken only between the generations, hinted that William had been the lover of a queen and had taken their son secretly at birth to be reared among his own children, an eagle among pigeons. The story must be true, else why would the castle, a royal seat, have been given to the Sedgeleys?

And above all, how explain himself? He had known long ago that he was no common man even among his peers. Proud he had been called, even arrogant, "that haughty young chap," they had said of him at Oxford, and the phrase had stung until he had told his father.

"And quite right," his father had said complacently. "You've every right to hold up your head. You're Sedgeley of Starborough Castle, and the rest of them are upstarts by comparison."

And yet, with all his pride, he was not free. He had the tenants—they had him! They were like their kind everywhere in the world, asserting not their independence but their dependence. The power of the weak! They were children, who demanded without thought of giving. Kings were their slaves as all rulers were slaves of the ruled.

The people were the tyrants, the discontented, dissatisfied, greedy, stupid people. If he had been an ordinary man, earning his living, even someone like Webster, would he be harried and oppressed as he was now, his conscience a burning coal in his breast because he felt responsible for his tenants as a king for his subjects? He groaned aloud. Intolerable burden laid upon him because he was born in a castle, the son of his father, heir to all the responsibilities of a kingdom! Well, it was a sort of kingdom—bigger than Monaco!

Musing thus as he did so often, Sir Richard now heard shouts. At the end of the winding road ahead he saw a ragged cluster of farmers waiting for him. There they were, wanting something again, he thought with deepening gloom, without the sense to know that the world as they knew it, and as their fathers before them had known it, was about to come to an end.

He quickened his horse to a trot and drew up before them, very straight and brusque. "Well, men? What do you want now?"

A rough fellow with a brush of tawny hair stepped forward and he recognized Banks, the troublemaker. "Please, Sir Richard, we've heard the castle's to be sold."

Sir Richard looked down at him from his seat on the great gray stallion. "Well?" he inquired coldly.

Banks looked back at him sturdily. "What's to become of us, sir?"

The question released the tongues of the others.

"Yes, Sir Richard—that's wot we wants to know—It's our bread, you know, sir—we've children to think of—"

Children! They had nothing but children swarming into the world for him to feed! The bitter injustice of it, that these British men could beget their British sons while he was childless—had always been childless, in reality, for how could a man in his position acknowledge a moment's madness when he was a mere boy—sixteen, to be exact. He stopped the memory, but not before a face appeared in his mind, a pretty face, a simple girlish face. He dismissed it instantly as he always did, angry that memory could be so relentless. His wife was his love, his only love, and yet when they argued as they had only the other morning, as to which was responsible for their childlessness, he saw that face, Elsie's face, and he sent it away. No, he could never reveal his secret. He could never retort to his wife, "I know I could have begotten a son—"

Nor had Elsie herself ever made a sign to anyone, even to him, that there was a secret, nor had Wells reminded him in all these years, though he must know—everything. Wells had been young then—older than himself by twenty years at that. Wells had simply announced one day that he and Elsie had been married the day before.

"At my request and for adequate compensation," his father had said sternly and refusing further explanation, had sent Richard off to Oxford.

"You have far too many children," he told Banks now.

The men burst into angry clamor. He lifted his hand to silence them and they stepped back.

"We have decided nothing," he said curtly.

He stared at them an instant, recognizing them one by one. James Dunn, whom he had hunted ferrets with as a boy, old Bumsley who had to be watched against poaching, Lester and Hunt and Frame, three of his best stalwart workers. His voice softened somewhat as he went on. "There's a great deal to be considered. We are mindful of you and your families. Lady Mary is as attached to the place as you could be. We know our position and you may be assured that we will look after your

welfare. We are aware of your troubles. Banks, we know
your roof wants thatching—"

There was an outcry.

"Tain't Banks alone, Sir Richard—"

"We've not had a new thatch since my grandfather's
time."

"Thatch—who wants thatch nowadays? A good slate
roof on every cottage, I say—"

"And septic tanks—"

The horse, startled at the noise, danced left and right
and rose to its hind legs. Sir Richard reined it in sternly.

"We are aware of all these matters. We have large
plans for the future. You will know of them in due time."

The men fell back as they always fell back when he
wore his kingly air.

"Thank you, Sir Richard—we know your hardships,
sir. Times is bad for us all. But with our families and all
—the women complaining about the leaks when it rains
—the children's beds have to be moved—damp runnin'
down the walls."

The broken chorus went on again until he stopped it.

"We know," he repeated grimly.

Banks put out his right hand.

"No 'ard feelin's!"

Sir Richard put out his left hand. Upon the forefinger
was his great seal ring. He did not wear it always, but
sometimes, as today, when he rode over his lands, he put
it on. The sight of it on his well-shaped hand was a
secret comfort, an invitation to dream. Nothing, no hard-
ship or confusion, could change the fact that he was born
Sir Richard Sedgeley of Starborough Castle.

Banks held the hand a moment. "A fine ring, Sir
Richard!"

"It was given to my ancestor, William Sedgeley, by the
king, five hundred years ago, when Starborough Castle

became ours. Castle and ring have belonged by right to every Sedgeley heir since that time."

There was a moment's silence. He knew what they were thinking. To whom would the castle go, and the ring, when there was no heir? Banks bent his head as though he were about to kiss the ring, and then dropped Sir Richard's hand. Did they know the secret? He'd wager they did. They knew everything, with their low cunning. It was part of their power over their rulers, to find out the secrets, the weaknesses, the youthful sins, the private follies, and use them when the time came.

He pressed his horse into a gallop and left the men staring after him. When he was out of their sight he pulled the ring from his forefinger and put it into the pocket of his coat. Then he reined his horse into a quiet trot again, and felt his lips tremble. Where could he find strength to sustain him, where gain wisdom to guide him? He was alone and lonely as only the rulers can be —must be, for how could he demean himself to ask from anyone the help he needed? There was no one his equal or, for that matter, his superior—no one living. Only his ancestors could give him courage, and to them he now turned.

He followed the road to Starborough village and to the church that had been built long ago for the devotions of a sovereign and his court. In it lay the dust of all the Sedgeleys since the day they had been given the right to lie there. He knew already where his own dust would lie —in that far corner to the east, where a shaft of sun fell through the prism of the rose window.

He dismounted, tied his horse to the hitching post and walked into the shadowy quiet of the church. It was empty and he strode up the aisle. Then he saw that it was not empty. The old vicar was standing before the altar, working at one of the tall silver candlesticks. He turned, startled, and put out his hand.

"Sir Richard, this is unexpected, but pleasant. I am just mending a bit of the candle here. One of the choirboys knocked it off during choir practice last night, but the candle's quite good if I can just . . . they are shockingly dear, these large altar candles . . ."

"Let me help you," Sir Richard said.

"Ah, don't trouble yourself," the vicar said. "Though I could do with a bit of help if you would just hold the candlestick . . . while I . . ."

Sir Richard grasped the heavy candlestick with both hands while the vicar lit a taper and held it to the candle to melt the wax enough to insert the broken bit. Sir Richard looked at the kind old face so near his own. He could remember the days when he was a boy and the vicar had come as a young man to Starborough village.

"As a matter of fact," he said, "I came here hoping for help for myself—not expecting you, of course—but just to—perhaps meditate a bit, near the graves of my ancestors. I am in great trouble."

The vicar did not look up. "Are you? I'm sorry to hear that, Sir Richard. Somehow I don't associate you with trouble. You've always been a good man."

"It's not that kind of trouble," Sir Richard said. "Nothing I've made for myself."

Nothing he had made for himself? Yes, it was hardly fair to call that brief episode on a lanquid summer's day, when he had met Elsie in the forest gathering wild strawberries, that hasty moment of physical excitement in a boy's body, a trouble that he had made for himself.

"Your seed is valuable—don't waste it," his father had said bluntly. "You're not only my son and heir. You're the son and heir of a noble line."

If his father had not been so crippled by war wounds, if he had been able to have other sons, how differently might he have spoken! But there was only himself, precious as the crown prince, his father's one hope of immortality. And had his father not pressed his ambition so heavily upon him, might not he, Richard, have been a different youth, less rebellious in heart, his repressed emotions less violent?

"Whatever your trouble is," the vicar was saying, "if I can help I'll be glad. . . . There—I think that'll hold. Set it down carefully, if you please, and we'll let the wax harden. Sit here in the choir stalls, Sir Richard, and tell me . . ."

But Sir Richard had wandered to the alcove where the Sedgeley tombs were placed. He was looking at the stone profile of William, in effigy on the central tomb, wearing his knight's armor. His stone hands were folded together in prayer, though he had been a warrior and not a praying man and there was little doubt, if the family records could be trusted, that it was true he had been the lover of a queen.

"I feel responsible for the castle," Sir Richard said slowly, gazing at the stone face, an arrogant face, even in death. "I am responsible," he went on resolutely, "for the castle and for the land that belongs to it and for the people upon the land. They look to me as their ancestors looked to mine. Yet I fear I can no longer hold my realm."

The vicar had followed and now stood with his hands folded under his robe. "I've heard a bit about that, Sir Richard. I'd hoped it was gossip."

"I wish it were. Unfortunately it is not. I shall have to sell the castle in order to save the land. There's no way out of it. An American is thinking of buying it, but . . ."

He paused and the vicar shook his head. "Oh dear, an American? Can't government—"

"Government's offered me a prison or an atomic plant —equally impossible! The castle is a treasure, committed to me. I can't save it. If I had an heir—but I don't. I'm a failure, I fear, as a ruler over my hereditary kingdom, if I may express it so. My people put their faith in me but I've not been able to— It's a strange story in its way, as strange as any of the tales of the castle in the old days."

"Tell it to me, Sir Richard. It will do you good."

"There was a king who took refuge in my castle— Charles the First. He'd lost London, he'd lost Sussex and he faced the loss of the throne," Sir Richard began. It was a story known to them both but always worth telling. "His people turned against him because he had failed them. People don't forgive a king. I lost London, too, you know—my own fault! My wife's often told me, 'You should have taken your rightful place in London'—that's what she's said how many times—and now it seems I've lost my Sussex, as well—and my own people. . . ." He kept staring down at the stone face as he talked. "I don't think it's ever been proved how Sir William died—some say he took poison. It doesn't matter. Let us say he took poison when it was discovered that he—" He put out his hand and touched the folded stone hands. "Damp," he muttered, "always damp. I remember when I was a boy. They were cold and wet."

"The church gets no sun," the vicar said.

Sir Richard seemed not to hear. He was muttering, half to himself. "He was betrayed by his own followers —betrayed to the King by someone who knew the story —his prime minister, I believe, a man whom he trusted. The prime minister knew about the child—a son, secret, of course."

The vicar looked at Sir Richard and put a hand on his arm. "Are you sure you're quite all right?"

Sir Richard shook the hand away impatiently. "Of course I am—why shouldn't I be? . . . It's all true. His wife never had a child. She blamed him. She insisted it was not her fault that they were childless. But he knew he could have a child—"

"I'm afraid I don't follow you, Sir Richard," the Vicar

said, bewildered. "How did he know he could have a child—whoever he is?"

Sir Richard turned to the vicar. His eyes were narrowed, his voice a whisper. "Because he'd had a child—by the queen! That's proof, isn't it?"

He gave a sudden shout of laughter, and then was as suddenly grave again. He moved abruptly away from the tomb and to the altar. He stood before it, staring up at the rose window, his back to the vicar.

"Tell me one thing—is there such a place as a home for souls?"

"I don't know, I'm sure," the vicar said gently. "Will you explain what you mean?"

"Well, you know—what if *they* really live there in the castle?"

"*They?*"

"My wife swears she hears *them*. And if *they* do, you know, what will *they* do if we take the castle down? Won't there be retribution—or some such thing—a disaster perhaps—for which again I'd be responsible, wouldn't I?"

The vicar stared at him. "Really, Sir Richard, you'd better have a cup of tea, and a bit of rest. Come to the vicarage and—"

Sir Richard did not hear him. "What would you do, for example, if this church were destroyed—through some failure of your own, say, which you did not intend, of course?"

"I would pray to be forgiven," the vicar said quietly, "and then I would continue my work under the open sky."

Sir Richard said no more. He left the vicar staring after him, and strode from the church, mounted his impatient horse and galloped away. Suddenly he felt the stab of fluttering pains inside his skull, now at his crown, then settling to throb dully behind his eyeballs. He would stop at the village inn and have a glass of ale.

... The long shadows of late afternoon fell across the stones when he approached the inn. The door was open and as he dismounted he heard loud voices, interrupted by derisive laughter. Some sort of argument was going on. He heard his name. He stopped by the hitching post and listened. The innkeeper—ah, yes, that was George Bowen's hoarse voice.

"I don't care what Sir Richard says! Get the hell out of here is what I say. Take it or leave it! Go home, you American chaps—we've had enough of you here—you and your kind! Fed up, that's wot we are! It's a sin and a shame to have to hear such talk—takin' the castle away from us! The Queen will never allow it, trust her!"

A friendly American voice made careless retort. "Don't get all steamed up, man! It's not up to us. We're hired to do the work, that's all. Anyway, the whole deal is off. Your precious Sir Richard threw us out."

"Thank God for Sir Richard, says I!" George bawled back at them. "He won't let us down, he won't! We'll have no tourists comin'—English kiddies wouldn't have no place to learn their own history if it wasn't for him and the castle. They come by the 'undreds—those London brats—"

The American voice broke in. "That's right—and you couldn't keep your inn open if they didn't."

Sir Richard could bear no more. He pulled the ring from his pocket, put it on his forefinger, and strode into the inn.

The innkeeper gave a shout of welcome. "Here he is, hisself, in the nick of time! Wot'll you 'ave, Sir Richard?"

"A glass of ale, thanks," he said coldly. He let his eyes move slowly from face to face. A few of his farmers were here, too, and they looked properly down when his eyes fell on them. Not so the Americans! They met his gaze with such smiling familiarity that he turned his back on them as he stood at the bar.

"Brazen and brass," George muttered. "I'd throw them out if they wasn't such good drinkers. I would that, Sir Richard, with all their talk of buyin' the castle and takin' it off to their own country! Invaders, I calls 'em—"

He was immensely fat and each year the space behind the counter grew more narrow for his spreading frame. He reached now to take a bottle from a special cupboard and gave a great gasp. "It's me or the counter—I can see that. I'll have to move it out or shrink myself down somehow."

"Hey, George," one of the young Americans shouted brashly, "what's that you're bringing out of hiding?"

George turned with difficulty but maintained his dignity. He opened the bottle and poured a glass of pale golden ale into a tall glass and set it before Sir Richard before replying.

"I'll thank Americans not to bandy my private name about," he said in a lofty voice. "Please to remember this is England and the gentleman sittin' here is Sir Richard Sedgeley, who owns the village and the land it stands on. In a manner of speakin', he owns us all. We look to him to defend us, like he always has and his ancestors before him. My family has lived here hundreds of years under the Sedgeleys and will live for hundreds more as I tells young George. . . . We thank you, Sir Richard."

Sir Richard inclined his head but did not speak. He lifted the glass of ale with his left hand, and the great ring shone upon his forefinger.

"Go to hell, Georgie," the American said, with a crass good humor. "I was here in the war but we weren't fighting you then and we aren't now. I even went with an English girl once—not steady, of course—too long in the tooth she was." He paused and inquired of his fellow Americans, "J'ever think she'd do anything about those teeth of hers? Have 'em out, I said, and I'll pay for the convenience. Get some store teeth that'll set back in your mouth, honey, out of my way. Do you think she would? No! And I bet she hasn't yet, though she could have 'em out now for free. Damned stubborn English—I sure was glad to go home."

"You couldn't be gladder than we were," George retorted. "And I'll thank you to be on your way home again—and the sooner the better. I want to get my place cleaned up, which I can't do until *you're* gone."

The American lifted his glass and downed its content. "Come on, fellows—there's nothing doing here. The loser is you, Georgie, when we're gone. Mr. John P. Blayne will simply put his money someplace else. . . . Good-bye, Mr. Sir Richard Sedgeley! Sorry we couldn't do business."

Sir Richard had stood by the counter all the while, drinking his ale slowly, giving no sign that he heard what was going on. Now he looked at the young American.

"It is not I who am dismissing you," he said coldly. "You work for Mr. Blayne, I believe. Did we not meet yesterday morning at the castle? I am not aware of—"

"There's a lot you aren't aware of," the man interrupted cheerfully as he sauntered toward the door. "So long, Georgie—good-bye, England!"

"Gangsters—that's what they are," the innkeeper declared when they were gone. "Good riddance, I say. Take your time, Sir Richard."

"I must be getting back to the castle," he said but he did not move.

The farmers lingering about the inn, some of them throwing darts now and again in a desultory fashion, began to wander toward the door. They had taken no part in the argument and as they passed Sir Richard they said nothing beyond muttered words.

"Evenin', Sir Richard—"

"We'll be on our way, sir—"

"My old woman will be hot to know what's become of me—"

"Our bit of supper will be waitin'—"

To each he gave a nod of recognition. Yes, he knew these, too, he knew their families, and had known them from his earliest memory when as a small boy he had ridden about the land with his father. He had his first horse, a black mare, he remembered, and it had given him a flush of pleasure when grown men stood as he passed and pulled their forelocks. The older ones still did so and he felt the same pleasure, deepened by the years of his responsibility—his reign, as he liked to think of it.

"Fill your glass again, Sir Richard?" George inquired.

"No, thanks, it is getting late." He paid for his ale and at the door looked back. "The Americans are right, you know, George," he said. "We are the losers nowadays, however we look at it. If the castle goes, would you rather have a prison or an atomic plant?"

George stared. "What's that, sir?"

Sir Richard tried to smile. "Tourists keep your inn going, but a castle—that's another matter. It takes more than tourists. . . . Mind how you behave with the Americans, George, when they come back. I fear that the deal, as they call it, is far from over."

He left then and George stood staring after him, his round eyes looking rounder than ever. His wife, a small thin woman with a long nose and scanty gray hair, came to the inner door.

"Supper's ready, George! What was all that rowin'? George, do you hear me? You look daft, standin' there!"

"It's him that's daft, I'm thinkin'," George said. "Sir

Richard has gone clean out of his mind, ravin' about prisons and atomics."

"You've been drinkin' all day," his wife said acidly. "Give over, do, and come and get something besides ale into that big belly of yours, where all the profit goes, I'm thinking!"

She disappeared and after a dazed moment, he followed. And beyond the village Sir Richard rode slowly homeward. He let the reins lie slack as he went and his eyes roved over the mellow landscape of field and forest. The afternoon light lengthened the shadows and deepened the gold of the willows and the green of growing wheat. In the distance the castle stood against the sunset in all its stately beauty. It was his home, his inheritance, and how could he give it up?

He tried to imagine the castle gone and over the low hills and broad valleys a magnificent modern farm with new machinery and farmhouses, his land tilled and productive, his barns rebuilt, a dream of a farm. In the distance he heard voices singing. The farmers were walking home by a nearby road. They had seen him riding along the road to the castle and too distant for greeting, they were singing, "For he's a jolly good fellow . . ."

He felt tears come into his eyes. They loved him. He raised his hand in acknowledgement as they went their way and echoes fell into silence. Yes, he could see the farm, the new beautiful farm made upon his ancient land, forests kempt and rich fields stretching into the horizon, and all his people happy again. But he—where would he be? How could he be happy, his castle gone? A king without a castle was no longer king.

His head throbbed in waves of piercing agony and he gave his horse a command. All that mattered now was to get back to his castle. The sun had dropped beneath the horizon and in the twilight the castle stood lonely and forlorn against the evening sky.

. . . "I'm sorry, Mr. Blayne," Kate said. "I shouldn't have called you to the telephone, but it was your father—from New York. At least it sounded like him."

He had been outside alone, watching the sun move slowly down the sky behind the towers, when he saw her standing in the open door of the great hall, her small figure distinct in a light dress the color of daffodils.

"How did it sound?" he asked, smiling.

"If I must speak the truth—like the bull of Bashan, roaring across the ocean!"

He shouted laughter as he followed her into the library. "That's my father." He took the receiver, "Hello! Hello?" No one answered. "He's hung up—probably sulking now because I wasn't here waiting for his call."

"Ah no, perhaps it's only a storm at sea." She took the receiver from his hand. "Operator, will you please get New York again? I have my party here waiting. . . . Very well, I'll keep him waiting."

She hung up and turned to him, her eyes dancing blue light. "She said she'd connect us again as soon as possible, but she has orders not to do so unless his blasted son was on. . . . Is your father always like this?"

"Always has been, always will be, bless him!"

"However did your mother—" She broke off and bit her lip. Impudence—what right had she to inquire?

"Stand it?" he finished for her. "She adored him and laughed at him and wasn't in the least afraid of him. Consequently he was utterly mad about her. When she died I thought he'd go insane. Everything she had owned became sacred. Nobody was to touch anything she'd touched. The paintings, for example, he wanted to lock them up."

"I like to hear about two people loving each other like that," she said quietly when he paused.

She stood leaning against the heavy mahogany desk, watching him. He took a small ivory elephant from the desk and when he did not speak she went on in the same quiet dreaming voice, her eyes on his hands—good hands, thin and strong and clean.

"Not that I know anything about such things, except what I've heard of my parents. My mother loved my father, or she'd never have married him. He was beneath her station." She hesitated, and then said shyly, "She was a lady, but I don't know why I keep telling you things."

He looked at her quickly. "Why shouldn't you tell me? I knew you weren't—what you've tried to make me believe you are."

"Oh, but I am," she insisted. "My father was the son of the butler here in the castle, remember?"

"Wells?" His voice was incredulous.

She nodded. "He is my grandfather."

They exchanged a long look and John Blayne turned away. "What does it matter?" he asked impatiently.

"I think it matters here in the castle," she said softly, "but not to me."

John Blayne began to pace the floor, acutely aware for the first time of why he was allowing himself to stay on in the castle. He wished she had not told him about her parents, and then he found himself wishing she would tell him more.

"What were they like, really?"

"From what I've been told," she began slowly, "my father was tall and handsome and very proud. I've seen ever so many pictures of him—as a boy—then after he grew up—then in his Air Force uniform. He never wanted to be a servant, so he ran away to London when he was twenty. He wanted to be an artist, and he even had an exhibition once in London. Most of his pictures were of the castle."

"Have you seen them?"

"No, they were destroyed in the blitz. Then he married and . . ." Her voice suddenly halted.

"And?"

"That's almost all there is to the story, except me."

"What was your mother like?"

"Her name was Diana Knowles. She was a lady, my grandfather always said, but I've never seen a picture of her and I gave up asking about her as my grandfather would tell me nothing. I think she was small and dark and slender and—distant-like."

"Why?"

"Because, for one thing, my grandfather told me her people were offish and that they didn't approve her connection with Colin Wells."

She had been looking anywhere but at him while she spoke, now she lifted her gaze and sought his. He smiled, then moved across the room to glance out of the window. Kate followed him with thoughtful eyes.

He was almost too handsome, she decided, as she watched him. One must be careful when one was a woman, especially a woman such as she, in a strange and anomalous position such as hers in the castle—at times almost a daughter, yet always the maid and grandchild of the butler.

Ah well, she thought wistfully, she had told him the truth. He had asked for it. Now that he knew it he could think what he liked. While she drove the sword thus into her heart she kept looking at him as he stood by the window against the background of the castle and the green lawns, a tall slender figure, elegant even in his casual gray slacks and jacket and his shirt open at the throat.

"You look like an Englishman," she said softly. "You could belong to the castle, standing there."

"I've been off and on in England all my life," he said. "My mother and I came in the summers quite often— we had a place in the Cotswolds—my father sold it when she died. He couldn't bear to see it again without her. They met in the Cotswolds, it seems—her family was English originally and came from that region."

"That explains you."

"It doesn't, as a matter of fact. I'm American—fundamentally and by choice."

"Now why do you insist upon that?" she demanded. "Is it a disgrace to be English?"

"Of course not, but I like American ways—the directness, the simplicity, even the selfishness, if you want to put it that way, an innocent sort of selfishness, I often think—like a child's. My father—" he broke off to laugh with a reluctant tenderness—"he knows what he wants and he sees to it that everyone else knows, too."

"Ah, but you're like that, you know," she said eagerly.

"I? Like my father? Come, now—"

"Yes, you are. You're well-spoken, and all that, but you've let us know what you want and I don't put it above you to get what you want in the end."

He had turned when she spoke and they were gazing sidewise into each other's eyes, half laughing. What a pretty thing she was, the way her dark hair curled about her head, the depths of the blue of her eyes, an English beauty, sprung from what contradictory roots! It would be difficult not to grow up beautiful here and yet not even the castle could have shaped the delicacy of her lips, the small straight nose, the finely etched brows.

He felt a dangerous pull at his heart, a rise in the temperature of his blood, and was alarmed. As if he had not complication enough now without allowing himself a romantic attachment, however temporary! He had long ago discovered that he was attractive to women and after an experience or two in college had developed a wary half-humorous technique for self-defense. Alas, the difficulty now was not to ward her off. He saw no sign of her approach to him. On the contrary, she had taken great care to insist that she was only the maid here in the castle, a notion which he was alarmed to discover was increasingly repulsive to him. He was disgustingly pleased to know that whatever her father had been, her mother— he checked himself. As if such distinction mattered in his own country!

No, what he must remember was Louise; and what he must ask himself was whether he had an obligation to her which he was honor bound to fulfill. His father and Louise's father were lifelong friends and business ene- mies. It had been taken for granted that the one's son and the other's daughter, who had played together as children, would some time be married. "A merger," the elder Blayne had called it.

Thinking about Louise, John realized that though he had often kissed her formally he had never kissed her spontaneously or uncontrollably as now, damn him, he could imagine himself kissing Kate!

He turned to her. "Was your mother a princess, by any chance?" he inquired with a desperate attempt at playfulness.

She sat down on the ottoman in front of the fireplace. "Perhaps . . ." She was about to say "entirely possible, one never knows about princesses," and then she checked the involuntary gaiety in her heart. "We began by talking about you," she reminded him, "not me. I was saying you are like your father."

"And I tell you I am not. Although . . ." He forgot her for a moment at this mention of his formidable father and stood looking down at her, hands in his pockets and frowning to remember. "I wanted to be like him when I was growing up. I tried to be interested in business, com- petition—all that—even football. I felt I was odd because I simply couldn't be interested in winning games. He always has to win, you know. Well, wanting to be like him, I had to resist him or he'd have ruled me like a slave. I have had to grow stubborn and argumentative in my own fashion—"

He broke off and looked down at her as though he had never seen her before.

"You're very clever," he said slowly. "Because you're right. In my own way I am like my father. Is that repulsive to you?"

She looked up at him, immensely tall above her, and was shocked to discover that she longed suddenly for— what? For his touch, for his hands to reach for hers to pull her gently to her feet, to . . . to . . .

"Oh no," she said quickly. "Not repulsive—of course not. I'd never have such a—a thought."

And what if he knew indeed what she was thinking? How could she save herself the shame if he knew that she dared not move lest she put out her hands to touch his?

"Irrelevant," he was saying, "but I never saw such eyes as yours. They're as deep as the sea, and darker."

She was silent, motionless, half hypnotized, and was delivered by the sudden sharp ring of the telephone.

"Oh," she gasped. "It'll be your father."

She slipped past him with profound relief, escaping the dangerous moment. How could I, she was thinking, how could I, when I'd never seen him until yesterday!

"Yes," she said aloud. "Yes, he's here. Indeed yes, Mr. Blayne. . . . Louise? No, I'm not Louise. . . . Yes, yes, he's been here this long while, waiting—"

She gave the receiver to him and tiptoed to the door, her heart suddenly cold. Louise? Who was Louise? Had he a sister? Or—she stopped, startled by a roar from the telephone.

"Johnny! Where in the devil are you? I've been trying to get you for the last six hours!"

The masterful voice bellowed its way under the Atlantic Ocean and shattered the peace of England. Wincing, he held the receiver as far from his ear as his arm could stretch.

"Yes, Father—yes. I've been waiting for hours, too."

He caught Kate at the door and frowned to her to come back. She stood waiting, in obedience.

"Who was that girl who answered?" the big voice shouted.

"She's somebody here at the castle," he said mildly. "Nobody you know—"

"Well, just don't forget Louise. I know a good merger when I see one. Holt called me that the old man doesn't want the castle moved and the deal's off. Crackpot idea from the first! Give my regards to Sir Richard and tell him I congratulate him on his good sense."

John Blayne's jaw set and his eyes flashed a pure steel. "The deal is not off. Holt has no business to say so! I don't give up—you ought to know that by now! If I don't get this castle I get another."

"And what about Louise? When I was young I didn't play ducks and drakes with a girl the way you are."

"Tell her—"

"Monday of next week is the day I've set for the merger to go through! Her father is coming from Pittsburgh with his lawyers. It's an occasion for the two firms as well as for the two families. I want you to be here, that's all—just be here!"

John Blayne exploded. "Listen, Dad, I take my job seriously! You made me responsible for the Foundation. If you don't like the way I'm running it, find someone else, but don't act as if it wasn't a job and as if you could send for me to come home any time you please— because you can't! The Foundation isn't a tax evasion scheme, so far as I'm concerned—it's a commitment to my mother's memory but even more than that, to the great works of art she left behind. You attend to your merger and I'll attend to my Foundation."

He was interrupted by an outburst of passion which, crossing the Atlantic Ocean, found vent in the crackling instrument in his hand. "Johnny, I've got a lot of money tied up in those"—the voice halted and went on—"in your mother's paintings! By the time you get your castles and whatnots, I can have a modern building put up and safe as Fort Knox—"

John stopped the loud voice by hanging up. His handsome face was crimson with rage. "Damn the old ——. I can always stay here in England, mind you! I swear I'll bring all the paintings here—and I will, if—"

Then he remembered Kate. "Sorry—excuse me—"

She was gazing at him with admiration. "You're as fine a man as your father," she said softly. "It would be hard to choose which has the bigger voice and the hotter temper. It was a real show!"

He gave a snort of laughter, short and grim. "I mean what I said. I'm not giving up. I'll go to France or Germany or anywhere, if it takes me years. . . . Monday in New York—to meet Louise and witness the merger! Merger—hah!"

Kate smoothed her skirt nicely over her knees.

"Who is Louise?" she asked in a voice so carefully casual that it was like the chance but piercing sting of a bee.

He was walking about the room and stopped by the chimney piece.

"Louise?" he repeated blankly.

"Yes, Louise," she repeated firmly.

"Louise . . . well . . ." he said slowly. "Louise is the daughter of a Pittsburgh coal millionaire and my father's best friend. For years they've planned to merge their companies. And our families have always wanted us to —merge, too. Coal, Louise; steel, me!"

He shrugged his shoulders elaborately and examined the painting above the chimney piece, a Romney duchess.

"She's a very wonderful girl and beautiful, et cetera—handsome is the word, I suppose—good clothes, always well turned out . . ."

He was thinking what to say, she could see that. And she could imagine Louise, one of those thin smart American girls—and what, pray, was this sudden ache under her breastbone, why was it so hard to breathe while she waited for him to speak? Oh Kate—you're a silly—

She spoke first, her voice small and strange. "You said you might stay in England—then why don't you leave the castle here where it was meant to be? You could have the museum here, which is what we thought you meant in the first place. Then we wouldn't all be torn to pieces."

He strolled to the window again and stood there, his back to her, and gazed out over the rolling hills and shallow valleys. A ray of the setting sun caught the spire of the church in the village and flashed it into a silver cross against the darkening sky.

"Plenty of reasons against it," he said impatiently. "Bring millions of dollars of paintings across the sea? Every crook in two continents would be on the alert . . . probably regulations between two countries about releasing works of art, besides. . . . There must be a solution, though, if I could only . . ."

He turned and sat down on a huge chest against the wall facing her and got up immediately.

"Handsome carving, but not to sit upon!"

She laughed suddenly at his rueful face. "King John's chest. He kept his valuables in it—a crown given him by the Scots and a gem-encrusted scepter."

He tried the lid. "It's locked—are they still there?"

"I don't know! The keys have been lost this long while. . . . What were you saying about a solution?"

He walked to the window once more and sat on the sill, his back to the landscape. "I was thinking aloud. . . . You know, I may be a silly idealist, but I really want the

American people to see something beautiful and not in a building on Fifth Avenue that looks like a washing machine. I want the paintings to hang in their authentic setting—a castle. We don't have a castle in New England —not a real one like this. It's an art treasure in itself. We Americans need this sort of thing . . . we've no sense of history. . . . Can you understand me, Kate?"

"This sort of thing," she knew meant the oak paneled walls, the huge chimney piece of stone built to burn eight-foot logs, the high, groined ceilings, the air of nobility, the atmosphere of ages.

"Please," she said softly, and all the time she was thinking how sweet it was to hear him call her Kate. "please never do anything you do not wish to do."

"That's easy. What's hard is to know what I do want to do."

The telephone rang before she could answer. She took up the receiver, listened, and handed it to him.

"For you—from the inn."

He heard a distant clamor of voices resolving into the voice of his lawyer.

"Yes, Holt," he said in reply. "Yes, I'm here at the castle. Everyone is to stay at the inn until I. . . . Yes, I have talked with my father. You should have waited for my instructions before— Yes, I know I must make up my mind. . . . I tell you, I don't care if there are thirty-five more people coming tomorrow! They can just wait, too. . . . I know you only want to be helpful—you're very efficient and I appreciate it, but efficiency must wait for something more important. . . . I don't know, I tell you. I'll have to think. . . . Yes, it'll cost a lot of money to wait, but. . . . All right, call it foolish, but foolishness in the beginning may lead to wisdom in the end— There *is* a solution, but I haven't quite— No, I don't know what we'll do—not yet! When I know, I'll tell you."

He hung up and turned to Kate. "Damned efficient idiot—"

She was not there. She had slipped away into the twilight as though she were made of mist. He strode from the room through the door where she had stood and went down a wide stone corridor into the far end of a passageway. The place was empty and his footsteps echoed as though he were alone in the castle. He looked about the vast spaces now sinking into the shadows of approaching night. By what outer door had she escaped and how could she have gone so far? He listened and imagined that he heard voices too distant to be recognized, a man's voice and then a soft answering voice. He went to the far end of the hall and opened a small wooden door bound in iron. It gave onto a short passage and there another door stood open, this one wide and heavy, and facing a wall. He went out and found himself in a dim street of cobblestone, stretching in both directions. At one end he saw a winding staircase of huge blocks of wood leading to an upper floor in one of the towers. Near the foot of the staircase two figures were silhouetted against the light of an old iron lantern swaying from a beam, the thin bent figure of Wells and near him Kate, leaning against a gnarled oak tree, her arms folded across her breast.

He stood for a moment, seeing them like ghosts in the setting of history. This narrow cobbled street between low stone buildings—here, he supposed, the servants of kings had lived, the maids surrounding queens and carrying on their secret hidden life in the vicinity of the great. Wells could have lived in any age, a thousand years ago as today, and Kate, who so short a time ago in the library had seemed miraculously near and real—it took no reach of the imagination to see her long ago in this very spot. He felt suddenly chilled and alien and was about to return to the great hall when she saw him. She nodded to Wells, who left her and went up the stairs while she walked sure-footed on the cobbles now growing damp with dew.

"Can I help you, Mr. Blayne?" she inquired as she drew near.

"No, thank you, Miss Wells," he replied.

"Then we had better go in. There's rain in the air."

She led the way and he could only follow until in the great hall they hesitated, she not knowing what to say, he determined not to speak. She moved to light the tall candles on the table. Her face was lovely in the flaring candlelight, a girl's face, very young and intent. . . . Twenty-four candles in all, he counted, and she was now on the fourth.

"And do you love Louise?" she asked, in a cool voice as controlled as the hand that held the long wax taper.

"That, Miss Wells, is not for me to say now, but what I shall say is that I am just beginning to know something about the difference between a merger and a marriage."

"I don't know what a merger is, at all," Kate said honestly.

Thirteen more candles to go. . . . She was lighting them slowly, taking pains to see that the wicks were cleaned of ash and that the flames burned bright.

"A merger," he said absently, his eyes upon the slender white hand that tended the candle, "a merger is the union of two firms. It has nothing to do with marriage, except in such cases as my own, where it happens there is a son in one firm and a daughter in the other. My father has the biggest steel company in—oh, hell, never mind. Her father has the biggest coal company. I told you all this, didn't I? And coal and steel—they go together like—love and marriage, as the song goes. Now you know what a merger is. Understand it?"

She lit the eighteenth candle. "Yes."

He stood up and leaned both hands on the table. "I'm glad you understand, for suddenly I don't. None of it makes any sense to me at this moment. Does it to you, really?"

She answered gravely, intent upon her task. "Yes, of course it does. . . . In England the prince marries the princess. Only it's not called a merger—it's called a marriage of convenience. Oh yes, we're quite accustomed to that sort of thing."

She lit the last candle as she spoke. He did not hear her. He was gazing at the lighted candles, her face glowing between them.

"Now, if you'll excuse me," she said, and lingered upon the question.

He sighed and straightened himself and stood for a moment, half-bewildered. How could he keep her here? How could he explain—but what had he to explain? His glance fell upon his briefcase, dropped when he came in and forgotten. He crossed the room and, hesitating, opened it.

"I have some photographs I brought to show Sir Richard," he murmured. "You might like to see them, too."

He came to the table where she stood watching him. He spread them before her. "They're Connecticut. The landscape isn't too different from England, as you see— a bit more rugged, perhaps—rocks and stone walls. The castle was to stand on this low hill above the river, the forest in the background. . . . There's the sketch. I made it myself, imaginary, of course."

She shuffled several sketches. "Here it is, the great hall. . . . Pretty good since I hadn't seen it, don't you think? Even to the chandelier—"

She saw the castle there in Connecticut as though it were a dream in a far country. The great hall was full of strangers, Americans, gazing up at the beamed ceiling. They were sketched in, tiny figures, blank faces.

"That chandelier," she said suddenly, "it isn't just a

chandelier, You'll have to be careful about people standing under it. It makes me shiver to think of it."

"Why?" he asked.

"It's dangerous," she said in a half whisper. "It has a voice, Lady Mary says. 'I'll drop it—I'll drop it.'" She imitated a faint far-off voice with a Scottish accent.

"Ah, don't laugh," she cried, when she saw him smile. "Lady Mary insists she's heard it."

At this he laughed aloud, diverted. "What an attraction for the tourists! And have you heard this voice?"

"No, but I've seen the chandelier shiver and shake until the crystals sing!"

"You're not serious!"

"Perhaps I am—"

"Come now—look into my eyes and tell me the truth!"

He seized her by the shoulders, still laughing. She was half laughing, by now, but before she could reply they heard the strong steps of booted feet and Sir Richard stopped in the doorway and stared at them. John Blayne dropped his hands and Kate stepped back.

"I've just put an idea to Mr. Blayne," she said.

"Indeed!" Sir Richard did not change his expression.

It was not enough to placate him, she could see, and she hurried on. "I suggested that he consider again the idea we had at first—to make the museum here, you know, Sir Richard."

Sir Richard lifted his heavy eyebrows, came in and stood beside them. "And what did he say this time?"

She glanced at John Blayne. "He refused again—not yet, anyway."

Before John Blayne could speak, Lady Mary entered. She had changed her tweed suit to a long gown of pale gray satin with a ruff of white lace and had touched her cheeks with rouge, a lovely, fading rose.

"Wherever have you been, Richard?" she inquired in her sweet childlike voice. "I've been fearfully worried about you. And what are you doing here? And in your riding things at this late hour? It's nearly time for dinner and Wells will be cross if we're late. We're dining in the small hall, Richard."

Sir Richard went to her and lifting her hand he kissed it gallantly. "I was about to look for you, my dear, to tell you I was home. Meanwhile, it seems, Kate has been bravely taking care of Mr. Blayne while you and I deserted the field. They've lighted all the candles because it's grown so dark they couldn't see each other. And Kate has made a proposal to him."

Lady Mary screamed delicately. "What? You're mad, Richard!"

Sir Richard put up his hand. "No, no—don't jump to conclusions! She proposed merely that he accept our original idea and bring the paintings here. The castle would become the museum where it stands, as we understood from the first."

"A splendid idea," Lady Mary said. "It always was. I can't think why you gave it up, Mr. Blayne."

John Blayne looked from one to the other of these three. Fantasy, he thought, dream people living in another age! How to bring them into reality! He began to speak slowly and clearly.

"Lady Mary, Sir Richard . . . and . . ." He looked at Kate and away again. "I wish I could agree that the idea is a good one, Lady Mary . . . it isn't, I'm afraid. The castle is too out-of-the-way here. It's not even on the tourist route from London." He hesitated a trifle awkwardly. Kate had turned away but Sir Richard and Lady Mary were looking at him with painful intensity. He must not hurt them! He went on, haltingly.

"Castles belong to a certain era, I suppose. They were necessary once, when a man had to build his own fortress. Today—well, fortresses don't protect any longer. They're rather like the Great Wall of China, where the people feared the enemy from the north. Now the enemy comes from the sky or the earth or the sea. We're surrounded! So the castle becomes a museum piece in itself, wherever it stands, in the old world or the new. The new world needs it more, perhaps—lacking a history of its own. Anyway, in this curious compressed world today, history belongs to everyone, everywhere."

Sir Richard rejected all this with a wave of the hand. "Socialism! My castle belongs to me, Mr. Blayne. Let us stay by the facts, if you please."

John Blayne turned to face him. "Very well—you shall have the facts, Sir Richard. My lawyers have investigated. Even with the castle open to the public for a year, one day of every week, you have cleared two hundred dollars or thereabouts. Let's see—that's about eighty-seven pounds. How many people? A few hundreds—enough to support an inn, I suppose, but not a castle. I'll be honest with all of you. It would be wrong, wouldn't it, to bring great works of art here, at immense cost, where no one would come to see them? . . . It wouldn't be fair—now would it?—to rob a new country like mine, whose people are hungry for art and beautiful things, by taking its treasures away and putting them where they couldn't be enjoyed by everybody."

He gazed at their faces and saw only uncommunicating gravity.

"Or am I wrong?" he inquired.

Lady Mary replied brightly to this. "What's wrong, pray, with an exclusive museum? It would be nice to have only people with clean boots. Put the idea to your father."

Sir Richard drew off his riding gloves. He was smiling now but vaguely, as though he were not listening, his eyes glazed and remote. He had withdrawn himself from them all. "Quite—quite," he murmured. His eyes fell on Lady Mary. "I see you're ready for dinner, my dear. You look very pretty. I expect Philip will soon be down. We'll join you in a few minutes. . . . Mr. Blayne, it's time to dress for dinner."

He left the room with dignity and after a moment John Blayne followed. He felt helpless. What could he do except leave them to their fate? And so he might have done, he realized, had it not been for Kate, so young and beautiful a creature whose fate and future were involved somehow with this ancient castle and the three dreamlike old creatures who inhabited it and would not leave it. As it was, what would become of her?

"Sir down, Kate," Lady Mary commanded when they were alone.

She sat down as she spoke in the great carved oak chair beside the chimney piece and folded her hands in her lap. She felt lost and alone. She, the mistress of Starborough Castle, was not being told what was really going on. Where had Richard gone riding for hours? Why had Kate been talking alone with the American? Who was plotting what, and she not told anything? The afternoon had been torturously long while she sat crocheting and in unbearable, tedious anxiety. Wells had been too agitated and irritable to question because of a guest for dinner and at last she had dressed half an hour too early, on the pretext that this gown, which she had not worn since she had been unable to afford her own maid, was difficult to get into alone.

"Now, Kate," she began. "What have you been saying to this young man?"

Kate sank on the hassock at Lady Mary's side. "I really said nothing, my lady, except that I do wish he'd just have the museum here as we wanted from the first."

"Quite absurd to think of it, as I now see him," Lady Mary said impatiently. "He's not the sort of person who could be at all happy here."

"Why not, please?"

"An American? Besides, Kate, I don't think *they* would

like it, you know—it would be so restricting to *them* to have an American about all the time, not to mention other Americans coming here, even in small numbers. *They'd* be quite put out. I shouldn't like to answer for the consequences. After all, *they've* been here much longer than we have, and *they* can't be ignored."

Kate reached for Lady Mary's hand, a slender nervous hand, delicately veined, restlessly moving. "Dear," she said, "are you quite sure you do hear *them*? It isn't just —dreaming? I sometimes think you live too solitary a life here, shutting yourself away even from the tourists."

Lady Mary withdrew the hand. "Certainly I hear *them*! And it's not only I, Kate. You remember what I told you about Richard's mother. She came here as a bride and the very first night in the castle, although simply nobody had told her about *them*, when she came downstairs to dinner she asked Richard's father who the lovely lady was at the top of the stairs. And old Sir Richard answered quite calmly, 'Ah, you've seen her! She was lady-in-waiting to a queen, and she was murdered by a groom who fell in love with her.' Certainly I don't dream, Kate, and it hurts me very much to have you doubt me."

"I don't doubt you, my lady. It's just that I myself can't see *them*—or hear *them*." She rose and stood beside Lady Mary.

"That means you do doubt them," Lady Mary retorted, "for if you believe in *them* you see *them*, or at least hear *them*. I do assure you, when I'm alone *they* make themselves known to me—put it that way."

"You don't actually see *them*?"

"I do see *them*, as clearly as those candles burn there on the table. Yet if you blow the candles out, quite possibly you might think they were never lighted, mightn't you? Or couldn't be lighted? They look dead until someone lights the flame. Well, that's how it is. When I'm alone, I concentrate for a moment, sometimes for half an hour, and I think about *them* and *they* feel me thinking and then *they* come out of the shadows. *They're* there, all the time, but *they* must be felt before *they* can be seen or heard."

She looked down at Kate wistfully. "Does that seem impossible to you?"

"Nothing seems impossible," Kate said softly. "I believe you. Have you ever talked to Sir Richard about *them?*"

"Of course," Lady Mary said. "Many times."

"And does he believe in *them?*"

"It's not a matter of belief with him," Lady Mary said. "It's a matter of seeing."

"If he sees *them,* why doesn't he speak of *them* as you do?" Kate asked.

"Perhaps we don't see the same ones," Lady Mary leaned to whisper. "What if he sees only bad ones?"

She looked over her shoulder and Kate saw a strange look of terror on her gentle face.

"Lady Mary, what's the matter, my dear?"

She seized Lady Mary's hands and held them in her own. They felt cold and limp and she chafed them. Lady Mary looked at her vaguely and answered, still whispering.

"I told Richard only yesterday that I thought there was a king in the castle, because the voice in the chandelier sounds as if it might be dear King John's voice. It's said he had a very strange high voice. And Richard said, yes, there was a king in the castle, but he looked at me so . . . so . . . darkly, somehow, that it couldn't have been the same king. . . . Perhaps he even saw one of the headless ones. I don't know. . . . I'm glad I see only the good ones. They're the ones that stay near me and want to help us."

"What did you say then, my lady?"

"I said, 'Richard, you do see *them* after all!' And he

said—and this was odd, Kate—very odd! He said, 'How would you like to be a queen?' "

"What did he mean?"

"Just that he didn't want to talk about it, I suppose. Whenever I want really to talk about *them*, he always talks about something else, to put me off. Oh dear—he can be very tiresome!"

She freed her hands gently from Kate's clasp and was silent for a moment before she began again. "Kate, I know that *they* can help us if *they* will."

"How?" Kate asked.

She was troubled by the conversation. All her life she had known that Lady Mary believed in these others who had lived in the castle and until now she had accepted the possibility of the persistence of the dead beyond life. England was an old country, crowded with history, and the castle was a symbol of the past. The bridge across the moat had been drawn up in many a fierce battle against Dane and Norman, and kings had found refuge here, princes been murdered, and queens taken to bed by their secret lovers. The castle was a storehouse of passion and revenge and ambition, retreat and inspiration. Whatever men and women had needed, they had created in their time. Only now, when the world had somehow got mixed into one great bewildering confusion, had the castle ceased to have meaning except for the handful of people who lived in it, of whom she was one.

And did she really live here? That telephone this afternoon from another world, that loud, commanding, arrogant voice of an American, how like the voice of an enemy it had seemed in the silent library, enclosed in book-lined walls—books that nobody read! Then was it the voice of life and today and a world from which she was hiding? No, not hiding! They needed her here in the castle, those two old dreamers whom she loved. Oh, if only she had been a man, she could have really helped

them! Instead, being a woman, she did not know what she
believed. Perhaps she had avoided knowing. She had
neither seen nor heard the dead but then she was busy
and young and strong. Lady Mary was often ill and spent
hours alone or with Sir Richard, and he could alternate
between calm good spirts, subdued and but a ghost of
what in his youth must have been a charming gaiety, to
moods of deep gloom, when he withdrew into himself or
even disappeared for hours together. At such times Lady
Mary was haunted with vague distress until he returned
again. It had been a long time since there had been
guests at the castle and it was true that when the public
came, Lady Mary shut herself away from them in her
private rooms to wait until they were gone.

"There must be treasure in the castle," Lady Mary was
saying. "In all these centuries someone must have hidden
jewels or silver and gold. Those kings and queens! *They*
know where it is. *They* will guide us to it, if we only
believe *they* will."

What could she say? She rose and stood looking at
Lady Mary and smiled half sadly. Then she put out her
hand. "Come, dear," she said tenderly, "it must be nearly
time for your dinner. The gentlemen will be waiting, and
I must change my clothes. My grandfather does not like
me to be late."

They walked arm in arm to the door. There Lady Mary
paused and turned to look back. "Put out the candles,
Kate. They cost two shillings apiece—those great wax
candles!"

She went on her way while Kate, obeying, took up the
heavy silver snuffer and snuffed out the candles, one by
one. The great hall sank into darkness and she stood lost
in its shadows, listening, feeling. The wind had risen after
sunset, the wind that had rain in it, and now it moaned
as it circled the towers and swept through the keep. There
was no sound of human voice or footstep. Believe, Lady

Mary had said, believe and help will come. But how does one compel belief and if compelled, is it true? She bent her head and clasped her hands together tightly under her chin and stared into the darkness.

"Help us," she whispered. "Please, all of *you*, any of *you*, someone!"

She waited a full minute and longer until she could not bear the sound of the lonely wind. There was no answer. Her hands dropped and she walked through the darkness toward the door that led upstairs to her room.

. . . In the small dining hall the three men waited for Lady Mary. It was a pleasant room at night, the crimson curtains drawn, a fire in the chimney piece, and the table lit for dinner. A silver bowl of rose-red tulips stood between tall silver candlesticks, and the tablecloth of Irish damask gleamed. Wells was serving sherry, and the men sipped their wine as they stood about the fire.

John Blayne held his glass to the light. "Liquid gold! How long have you had this, Sir Richard?"

"I haven't replenished the cellars since the war," Sir Richard replied.

"If the cellars are full of this sort of thing, you needn't sell the castle," Philip Webster said, and smacked his lips.

"Ah, but they're not full," Sir Richard retorted. "They're all but empty, like everything else."

"I suppose you haven't thought of selling the other treasures," Webster went on.

"No," Sir Richard said shortly. "I haven't the right."

"Who but you has the right?" Webster countered.

"There are other inhabitants," Sir Richard replied.

John Blayne lifted his handsome brows. "You mean—"

"I mean the figures of history," Sir Richard said.

"Not ghosts?" Webster asked, half teasing.

"The great dead," Sir Richard said gravely.

Lady Mary stood at the door, a graceful slender figure in her silver-gray gown. "Have I kept you waiting?"

"No, my dear," Sir Richard went forward and took her hand with old-fashioned grace. "We're having a drop of sherry and making idle talk."

He pulled out her chair for her and took his own place at the head of the table.

"You're at Lady Mary's right, Mr. Blayne—Philip at her left."

They sat down and Wells served the soup from a tureen on the buffet. John Blayne looked about the room.

"Where's Kate?"

The silence was broken by Wells saying apologetically, "She will be here presently. Something made her late this evening. I am sorry, my lady."

Webster tasted the soup, then tucked his large linen napkin into his collar and said briskly, "Excellent soup, Lady Mary."

"Yes, Wells does nicely with his soups. I believe he uses bones," Lady Mary said. She supped her soup daintily, barely touching the old silver spoon to her lips. In the glow of the candlelight her pale face was faintly pink and her eyes were mystic.

John Blayne pursued the subject of Kate with dogged determination. "Kate is a sort of secretary, isn't she?"

"Quite indispensable whatever she is," Lady Mary said gently.

"Also quite beautiful," John Blayne suggested.

Wells turned to face the table. Without looking at any of them, as remotely as though he were introducing a stranger, he spoke.

"My granddaughter is the maid, sir." And with the announcement, he left the room.

"I am glad you two gentlemen are to stay the night," Sir Richard remarked as though he had not been listening. "I never like to discuss business after dinner. It will be much better in the morning—especially as the day has been somewhat exhausting."

"Always a pleasure," Philip Webster said.

"Thank you, Sir Richard," John Blayne said. "You know, I haven't had a look at the castle yet. I'd like to have a real tour—not for any business reasons but simply because it's the most enchanting place I've ever seen— enchanting and enchanted. I'm sure that anything could happen here."

Lady Mary leaned forward, her face alight. "Do you really think so? Then it can. It's all a matter of belief— what the good book calls faith. I assure you, I have myself seen—"

"Please, Sir Richard."

Kate was at the door. She had changed into her black dress, with trim little apron and cap. She had brushed her hair freshly and washed her face in cold water. John Blayne saw her standing in the dark doorway and could not take his eyes from her. Last night he had accepted her attire as that of someone playing a part; tonight it annoyed him. He found himself in rebellion against the indulgence of class distinction. In America, Kate would have made her own way whatever her family connections might have been.

"There's a call from New York," she was saying. "I think it's Mr. Blayne's father again, sir."

He got to his feet and dropped his napkin on the table. "My father? I can't imagine what more he has to say to me—he said everything an hour ago. Do excuse me, Lady Mary."

Lady Mary looked startled. "Oh, of course—but fancy hearing someone speak across the sea!" She watched the two young people disappear into the dark passage, then continued. "Richard, I can't think why you feel it's strange I hear *them* speak, from beyond, especially when someone far away can speak to us here in the castle, no wires or anything connecting—and he a perfect stranger and an American, at that!"

"I don't think anything is strange, these days," Sir Richard said absently.

Wells entered with roasted grouse on a silver platter.

"Delicious!" Webster exclaimed. "My favorite game. But it's not in season."

"If you please, sir," Wells said firmly. He served the small birds and dripped bread sauce on each.

Webster laughed. "Very well—I won't ask. A man has a right to his own grouse."

"I won't have poaching, Wells!" Sir Richard exclaimed.

"No, sir," Wells said. "That's what I told the poacher when I took the birds away from him."

"You should have given them over to the game warden, Wells," Lady Mary said reproachfully.

"We may as well eat them as the game warden, I daresay," Webster said cheerfully. "At least now that they're here."

"Yes, sir," Wells said and left the room again.

They ate in silence for a moment. Webster took a delicate bone in his fingers and nibbled the meat with relish and put the bone down again and wiped his fingers on his napkin. "I must tell you, while our guest is out of the room," he said, "that I have made one more desperate effort for the castle as a national treasure. Castles are aplenty—did you see the advertisement last week in the *Times*? A castle with two hundred and fifty rooms and ten baths to let for a shilling a year—and upkeep, of course, which is twenty thousand pounds. True, there aren't many castles a thousand years old. I haven't much hope, yet there's a straw of a chance. I'm glad you asked Blayne to stay over, Richard."

"I feel sure something will happen," Lady Mary said.

Webster picked the tiny bird clean and now sat back to

wait for the joint. "What, Lady Mary, can possibly happen?"

"Something will happen," Lady Mary repeated. Her gentle blue eyes were remote, a faint smile moved her lips. She had only toyed with the bird on her plate and now she gave up pretense of eating. The diamond rings on her restless hands glittered in the candlelight as she put knife and fork together on the plate. "I have faith that it will," she said.

"It may, indeed," Sir Richard said absently. "It is quite possible—the divine right of kings."

Webster looked from one old face to the other in amazement. "Is there something here that I don't understand?"

Neither of them replied and Wells entered with the joint, set the tray on the buffet and began delicately to carve large, thin slices.

"Mr. Webster likes his beef rare, Wells," Lady Mary said.

"Yes, my lady," Wells replied. "I know, my lady."

"Oh, you always know everything, Wells," Lady Mary complained.

. . . In the library, John Blayne held the receiver as far as possible from his ear and Kate stood in the doorway, laughing softly to herself.

"Listen to him," he muttered, catching her eye.

"I can't help hearing him," Kate replied. "You should have said nothing to him about putting the museum here. He'll have an apoplexy. It was naughty of you when you don't really want it here yourself."

John Blayne bit his lip and winced as the relentless voice roared on.

"What do you mean by hanging up on me, damn you? I haven't been able to get you back to tell you. You're out of your mind. You oughtn't to be allowed to go around alone, Johnny! I wouldn't let those paintings out of the country—not for nothing! I shan't give them to anybody, either, not even to the Metropolitan—I paid good money for them! I'll cancel the Foundation first."

John Blayne glanced at Kate again and swung his arm round and round, windmill fashion, pretending to wind up his courage. Then he bellowed into the telephone.

"My turn, Dad! Hear this—I'm talking! I agree with you! . . . How's that? Yes, I said I agree with you. Ah—"

He gave a gust of a sigh as silence fell and went on again. "Yes, I know you don't know what to make of it . . . I agree with you, but for different reasons. Not because you paid good money for them, though money is always good. Not because it's wicked to give anything away because it isn't . . . Yes, I'm saying I agree with you! . . . Yes, and I agree with you because I want people to see the pictures every day and all day long, including Sundays and holidays, and that's why I want them kept in Connecticut, as near as possible to several great cities, and with good roads coming and going, and comfortable chairs to sit on where people can rest and look at the same time. And people can't come here, so we won't bring the paintings here— What's that? Are you having a thunderstorm there in New York? . . . Oh, you're just telling me to shut up! . . . All right, sir. Goodbye—but with love. . . . Hear that, Dad? I'm signing off —with love, Johnny!"

He hung up and burst into loud laughter. "Oh God, what a parent—what an irrepressible, inextinguishable, lovable old devil of a parent!"

His eye caught the picture of her again standing there in her incredible costume. He put his hands in his pockets to keep them safe and sauntered toward her. "I have an idea. *You* can help me!"

She looked up at him, her face shining with laughter. "*Can* I isn't the question. It's *will* I—"

"Ah, but you will—you must!"

"If I must, I must, I suppose—but still only if I wish!"

"Then persuade Sir Richard to let me have the castle, Kate—and you with it!"

"Me—like a piece of furniture?" She had stopped laughing.

"I could never get the castle together again without you," he said. He saw the look on her face, doubting, puzzled—wounded?—and went on hastily. "You can be a special consultant or something—anything you like."

She drew back a step.

"I'll pay you," he said, following her. "I'll pay you anything you want."

"Pay me?" she repeated. "You couldn't pay me . . . I'm not for sale . . . any more than the castle is. Oh no, you don't know me at all . . . I'm not in the least . . . what you think I am."

She walked away from him across the dim room to the window and he stood staring after her and saw for the first time the smooth white nape of her neck, under the feathery dark curls. But what had he said to make her angry? The moon had risen, an early moon, doing its best to show through the low scudding clouds; its pale light fell upon her in the huge dimly lit room. She turned to face him.

"You have no conception of the castle and what it means," she said earnestly. "This is a world, this castle! It's not stones and furniture—it's history, lived by people. You can't buy history or move it to a new country. You can't buy the people who have lived in it nor can you move them. . . . You're a merchant after all, Mr. Blayne. You have no feelings. Lady Mary is right. One has to feel before you can know. You only know what you can count and see, but she knows much, much more.

She has an influence here. And there must be another way."

He kept his distance, watching her. How strange she was! Who was she? Not the English girl he had been with an hour ago, not the girl laughing at him even a few minutes ago! How had he lost her?

She turned away again to the window and looked at the moon. He came to her side and saw her face pale and beautiful and remote. Whoever she was, he could never forget her now. He was half afraid of her, drawn to her, yearning to touch her, to have her back again, and yet he knew he could not unless and except by her own wish. Did she herself know who she was? A foundling perhaps, a child of royal blood left here somehow, not belonging to Wells—oh, certainly never belonging to Wells. There was not the slightest resemblance to him in this pure profile, this slender grace of her small head held so proudly.

"Please go away," she was saying. "Go away and leave us to our castle and to our times. Leave us above all to ourselves! We have lived here a long time in peace and loneliness. Go to your own new country where you belong and let us stay here in our old country where we belong."

"Kate," he said, "Kate, are you dreaming too?"

"No," she said quietly. "I never dream."

She would not turn to look at him. He waited and still she refused herself to him and he left her, after a moment, there by the window in the moonlight.

. . . He was glad, somehow, to return to the warm fire-lit room, where Sir Richard and Lady Mary and Webster were eating roast beef and potatoes and boiled cabbage.

Philip Webster was reading a telegram. He looked up as John Blayne took his seat.

"I'm afraid there's no hope, Sir Richard," he was saying. "It seems they can't consider adding the expense of another castle just now. Three million unemployed, et cetera—some eight thousand more elementary schools needed and so on—" He broke off.

"Am I interrupting something?" John Blayne inquired.

"Not at all," Sir Richard said. "We've no secrets at this late stage. . . . Go on, Webster! Government considers everything more important these days than castles a thousand years old."

Lady Mary gave up eating roast beef and put her knife and fork neatly together on her plate. "There is another way, Philip."

"Surely you don't mean ghosts again, Lady Mary," John Blayne said cheerfully.

Wells put hot roast beef before him, served potatoes and cabbage and went out again.

"Never," Lady Mary said. Her delicate face went pink. "I hate that word! *They're* spirits, more real than we are here. Don't call *them* ghosts—not in my presence, if you please! *They're* alive. This is *their* home and it can't be taken away from *them*. *They* do exist. Richard, speak up for once! *They* exist . . . you know *they* do, don't you? Don't *they?* Answer yes or no!"

Sir Richard sipped his red wine and wiped his lips carefully. "Well, my dear, I can only say that in any case I am not responsible for *them*. I'm only responsible for you and me and the land and my tenants. I must make my decisions on tangible things."

"Very well!" Lady Mary retorted. "Give me a few days, all of you. There are a hundred and fifty rooms in this castle, places we've never seen—hidden treasures, perhaps!"

John Blayne laughed, relieved at the vigor in the air. He'd bait her a bit more, just to enliven the meal. "Oh, come now, Lady Mary! You can't be serious. Every castle has these treasure stories."

Lady Mary looked at him with her calm gaze. "I'm not sure it's worthwhile, but I will explain. Whether you can understand is another matter. One has to be—I don't know how to put it except to say 'pure in heart,' if one is to see *them*—the good ones, I mean, the ones who will help. Otherwise the bad ones can take one over completely—use one, you know."

"Lady Mary," John Blayne said, "you mystify me. In everyday words, I haven't the least idea what you're talking about."

"Ah, you aren't trying," she said. "You must be willing to learn how to feel beyond yourself. You must give yourself up. Then you will hear sounds you have not heard before—perhaps just one sound, a clear high note of unchanging music. You will see—I don't know how to put it, but it's like looking through a long tunnel and seeing at the far end a small shining light. Concentrate on the light with all your being—and then ask for what you need. You may see someone—or not see—but you will get an answer—or perhaps just a feeling of peace and relief. But if you don't see or hear, then wait. In a few days, perhaps—"

She met his unbelieving eyes and she smiled faintly. "You don't understand, poor man, do you? But it's true for all that. In countries older than ours, in Asia, it's well known. It's called *prana* and there've been many books written about it. It's not ghosts or any of that nonsense, it's simply learning how to enter another level of being. You must want to learn how, of course—and for that, one must long for something—have a need before one can ask that it be fulfilled. And then— Ah well, we each have to do our own asking."

She spoke with such simplicity, such conviction, that he was unwillingly moved and reminded, to his surprise, of a conversation he had had with the aged minister who had officiated at his mother's funeral.

"She was a good woman," the old man had said, that quiet autumn evening beside the newly made grave, when all others save himself and the minister were gone. "But what interested me was her delicately perceptive mind. She was universal in life and she will be eternal in death."

"What do you mean?" he had begged, longing at that moment of fresh bereavement to believe that his mother was not beyond his reach. Did the dead still live? At that moment in the silent churchyard he could almost believe.

The minister had hesitated, his thin face flushing. "I can only say that by faith I arrive at possibilities that I believe scientists will one day confirm. In short, my dear boy, I have faith that death concerns only the body. Your mother pursues her way with her usual gaiety, but on a wave length of her own, if I may pretend to scientific knowledge I don't actually possess."

John Blayne turned now to Sir Richard, who had sat listening, sipping his wine, his expression remote.

"Sir Richard, do you believe as your wife does?"

Sir Richard put down his glass and touched his moustache with his napkin. "Well, there've been twenty generations of kings in the castle and a couple of queens, not to mention five centuries of my own family. Who am I to say that my wife is wrong? Only last year I found a ruby in the tennis court. I certainly didn't put it there. I'd never seen it before. We've never looked for treasure."

"Or asked for it," Lady Mary put in.

"Or asked for it," Sir Richard agreed. "But stay a few days, and you'll see for yourself."

"Thank you," John Blayne said. He felt suddenly confused, yet unwilling to yield to a vague but mounting uneasiness. He had long ago given up his secret half-shamed attempts at communication with his mother. He had accepted, as he would have put it, the fact of death, perhaps total. Here the line between life and death was not so clear, but he did not propose to be drawn into that morass again. "I will stay," he said briskly, "if you'll let me proceed with the survey. . . . I don't believe you'll find the treasure—not in the way you're looking for it, although it's quite possible that if we take the castle apart, stone by stone—"

Lady Mary rose abruptly. "Pray excuse me," she said and left the room.

The three men sat in silence for a long moment. It became unendurable and John Blayne broke it.

"Lady Mary is charming in her earnestness, Sir Richard —but these old fancies—"

He paused and Sir Richard did not look up. He had taken his wineglass again and was twisting it slowly in his fingers, gazing into its deep color, blood-red against the candlelight.

"You don't believe in *them*," he said at last.

"Do you?" John Blayne countered.

Sir Richard shrugged slightly and lifted the decanter. "A little more port? No? . . . Webster?"

"No, thanks," Webster said. "And if you'll excuse me I'll go to bed. It's been a long day."

"For all of us," John Blayne agreed. He felt stopped, as though suddenly a door had closed against him.

They rose and Sir Richard pulled the bell rope for Wells.

"Take the gentlemen to their rooms," he ordered.

"Not me," Webster said. "I know my own way about. Good night, Richard."

"I'll say good night, too, Sir Richard," John Blayne added.

He was not sure that Sir Richard heard. Webster was gone and he stood by the dying fire, abstracted, his head bent.

"This way, please, Mr. Blayne," Wells said.

He could only follow. The passages were no longer quite new to him now, particularly those that led away from the great hall and the front of the castle toward the east wing; but he felt that he could easily become lost. The floors were of gray stone, uncarpeted, and the windows were narrow and deep-set. The walls, he reflected, must be three feet thick. He caught up with Wells.

"Do you believe in these ghost stories, Wells?"

Wells did not turn his head or slacken his pace. "I never listen to what's said at table, sir."

"Even though you're in the room?"

"No, Mr. Blayne."

"And how long have you lived here?"

"All my life, sir." He paused at an oaken table at the foot of a stairway and lit a candle which was standing there.

"We go up two flights, if you please, sir, to reach the Duke's room from this side of the castle."

"The Duke of what, by the way?"

"The Duke of Starborough, sir. He was a protégé of Richard the Second, I believe. His room is not so damp as some on the lower floors. And I expect you have enjoyed the view of the river and the village when you look out in the morning."

"Indeed, I have."

They were climbing a short flight of worn stone steps and now stopped before the familiar door. Wells twisted the brass knob. The door creaked but did not yield. The flame of the candle fluttered in a sudden gust of wind.

"The windows must be open," John said.

"Indeed, no, sir," Wells said. "There's always a gust of wind when one comes to this room at night."

"Why is that?"

"I can't say, sir. It's always been so— There, the candle's gone out. Stand still, if you please, sir. I always carry matches."

John Blayne stopped in the darkness. He heard a howl of wind under the door and the scratch of the match. The candle flamed again. Wells was standing with his back to the door, shielding the candle.

"Hold the candle for me, please, sir," Wells said under his breath. "I'll back in and then I'll have to keep the door from slamming on us. Hold the candle close to me, sir, and don't make a noise."

John Blayne laughed somewhat unsteadily as he took the candle. "Are you playing some sort of game, Wells?"

They were in the room now. The door slammed and the candle went out again as though fingers had pinched it. In the darkness he heard Wells muttering. "Oh, you tiresome creatures! . . . Let's have no more of this nonsense. . . . Here, sir, give me the candle, if you please. I'll set it to the table."

He felt Wells' fingers, cold and damp, fumbling at his own hands and he yielded the candle hastily and stood in the darkness waiting. The air was still and whatever the wind was, it had ceased. He heard the scratch of the match and once more the candle flared. This time it burned.

"There," Wells said in triumph. "You'll have no more trouble now, sir. *They* know when I mean what I say. . . ."

"*They?*"

"Yes, sir. *Them*, you know. *They* won't bother a stranger, sir. It's only us whom *they* know that *they* tease —maybe it's only the children, at that. A lot of children died young in the early days, I daresay—here in the castle, too."

Children? What was the old man saying?

"If the candle gives you any trouble, sir, there is the electric light by your bed. There now," he chatted amiably as he moved about the room, "I've turned down the bed, sir, and I put in a hot-water bottle against the sheets being damp—a stone pig, we call it. It'll keep warm all night. There's no bath here in the east wing,

I'm sorry to say, sir, but I'll fetch a portable tub in the morning and a tin of hot water, when Kate brings in your tea and toast. . . . Good night, sir."

He was at the door and he paused to look back. There was no wind now and the candle burned steadily, its glow aided by that of the shaded lamp by the bed.

"I hope the chapel bells won't wake you, sir. They often sound at four o'clock."

"Chapel? Ah yes, she told me—your—"

He broke off, not knowing how to speak of Kate, but Wells went on smoothly.

"The big ballroom, sir, just under this room, was the chapel when the castle was a royal seat. Some people can hear the bells—I often do, myself. So does Lady Mary. Sir Richard does too, I think, but he'll never say. Good night again, Mr. Blayne."

The heavy door swung shut with a screeching creak and silence fell, the deepest silence that John Blayne thought he had ever known—felt, rather, for he could imagine it almost solid about him. What was it Lady Mary had said? Feel, she had said, and then concentrate on the light at the end of the tunnel, the distant small light, and ask for what was needed. Nonsense, as if he needed anything that he did not have! And yet—and yet—he was beginning to feel that there was something he very much wanted, something that money could not purchase.

He undressed and went to the old-fashioned stand. The huge silver jug standing in the big porcelain basin was full of hot water. He filled the basin, wrung out the steaming washcloth and washed himself all over before he put on his pajamas. It was the sort of thing, he supposed, half humorously, that even kings and queens had done once upon a time, not to mention dukes.

"Not bad, Duke, old boy," he said aloud and suddenly was in such good humor that he began to whistle softly.

He blew out the candle but placed it carefully on the stand by his bed in case the electricity should fail.

"For he's a jolly good fellow—" He climbed into an enormous bed, raised under a canopy of crimson satin, and then remembered he had left the matches on the table. He'd better have the matches, just in case.

"In case you show up, Duke," he said conversationally, "and try your tricks again."

Once more in bed he settled himself deep into the soft mattress and the enormous down-filled pillows. A faint smell of mildew reminded him of an ancient odor he had smelled elsewhere. He sniffed, trying to remember. Ah yes, Cambodia and the ruins of Angkor! The hotel bed there had had the same faint reek of time and decay. And he had imagined those ruins haunted, too, not by anything as preposterous as ghosts, yet by something as vague, a presence accumulated through centuries of compressed human life. Was it not possible, even inevitable, that the material of the human body, the mass, must leave behind a transmigrating energy?

He felt now as he mused, an uncomfortable awareness, a pressure almost physical, which chilled him, and with something like panic he laughed aloud at himself and ceased his imagining. Let him think of something pleasant at the end of this second curious day! Too much had happened to him in too few hours and what was the most pleasant sight he had seen? Unbidden, he saw Kate smiling at him out of the darkness—a pretty face, sweet and unspoiled, the blue eyes honest and warm. A talisman, proof against dead kings and queens and whimsical dukes, he told himself, and fell asleep upon the comforting thought.

Part Two

~~~

. . . LADY MARY stirred in her wide canopied bed. She opened her eyes and gazed into the darkness and lay motionless. Something had wakened her, a noise, a voice, perhaps. Had Richard called her? She sat up, yawned delicately behind her hand and switched on the lamp on her bedside table. The white curtains at the windows were billowing gently into the room and the air was damp. The expected rain had come and now there must be fog rising from the river. She turned back the blankets and felt for her satin slippers on the floor. She must go at once and see if Richard wanted something. Slipping into her white negligee, she lit the candle to guide her through the passage between her room and Sir Richard's, the passage that had no light otherwise, and pattered softly through it. Both doors swung open easily, she entered his room and going to the bed, she stood looking down at him, shielding the flickering light of the candle from his face with her hand, lest he awake.

"Richard," she whispered.

He did not answer. He was asleep, his breathing deep and steady. It was not he, then, who had called. Who could have waked her? She tiptoed out of the room and into her own again, closing the doors. Should she go back to bed? She hesitated, shivering in the damp air. Then as always when she was undecided she gave herself up to concentration, standing with her eyes closed, until at the far end of the long tunnel she saw the shining light of awareness of what she should do. . . .

The familiar sense of ease, of relief, warmed her body. No, she was not to go back to bed. Put on something warm, her flannel robe, and what then? Just walk about, perhaps, feeling everything, feeling it to be the right moment, perhaps waiting until *they* told her? She might not hear a voice, but sometimes she was moved by feeling, as though unseen hands, lighter than the mist, were touching her cheeks, her hands, her shoulders, guiding her somewhere. Yes, now she could feel *them*, leading her down the passage and the corridor to the great hall. She yielded herself until at last she stood under the chandelier, and felt herself stopped. Wait, she felt, wait to hear a voice, King John's voice, if it were his, poor King John. He had always been one of her favorites, nevertheless. She had come across a description of him once in an old book in the library.

Tall and fair of body, with fierce blue eyes and ruddy fair hair; voracious, always hungered, a young man coming late to love, and having no shame in drinking all day and all night—

It had made her think of Richard when they fell in love—"coming late to love," so late that she had wondered if there had been a woman before her. She had not dared to ask, and for awhile had been eaten up with unspoken jealousy because he told her nothing of an earlier love. She looked up expectantly into the chandelier and saw the crystals twinkling and shining faintly in the candlelight, like a face with a thousand eyes.

"Very well," she said softly, "if it's the moment then

say something—please, King John, tell me where the treasure is!"

She gazed upward, head thrown back, her long silvery hair streaming down her back and listened, her face intent.

"Or what is it?" she whispered into the light.

. . . Kate was asleep, too, but lightly. She had left a candle burning on her dressing table, a small candle set into a deep bowl against possible fire. She kept a candle always burning lest Lady Mary call her at night. She lay quietly now as she slept, her dark hair loosely curling on the pillow, and her bare arm flung upward about her head. The other hand lay open, palm upward, on her breast. She was beautiful asleep, though no one was there to see her, half smiling, dreaming of recent adventures, the lily pond and the sunshine, the firelight in the great hall and John's tall figure at the window.

A door creaked and her eyes opened. She waked at the slightest sound, aware even in her sleep of the two for whom she felt responsible because she loved them.

"Yes?" she called.

No one answered. She raised herself on her elbow and saw a dark silhouette, a shadow at the door. She caught her breath, stopping with her hand to her mouth the sound that might have come involuntarily. Lady Mary came into the room.

"It's only I, Kate. My candle went out and I'd forgotten to put the box of matches in my pocket."

She walked to the bed and looked down into Kate's wide eyes. "What's the matter, child? Have you seen something, too?"

"No, my lady—only I wasn't expecting to see you."

"I wasn't expecting to be here," Lady Mary said, "but I was called. I got up and waited for instructions and now it's quite clear to me, Kate, that this is the right moment for us to act."

Kate, gazing up at Lady Mary, felt suddenly afraid—of what? Not of this gentle aging figure, surely, whom she knew better than she knew her own impulsive self, she sometimes thought, except that Lady Mary looked at this moment so transparent, so fragile, so unearthly, that she—

"Have you heard a voice, my lady?"

"I don't know," Lady Mary replied. "I think I did hear someone, but I can't be sure I really heard anything—or anyone. I was simply pervaded, if you know what I mean—"

"I don't, quite," Kate said, wondering.

Lady Mary was a trifle impatient. "I can't stand here explaining, Kate. It's simply that I feel *them*. I know *they* are moving about. There's excitement. Get up at once, Kate. *They* can be very difficult if *they* are wanting to tell us something and don't find us waiting. *They* will go off in a huff. It's quite difficult for *them* to reach us, you know. I daresay *they* try as hard as we do."

Kate reached for her rose-colored dressing gown. She smoothed back her tumbled hair and tried not to shiver. Lady Mary did look strange—resolute, grave, but remote, especially her eyes—

"Shouldn't we take someone with us, my lady?" Kate asked. "I'll call Grandfather, shan't I?"

"Certainly not," Lady Mary said. "He's much too old. We don't know where we'll be led—perhaps into the dungeons. He might slip on those wet stones and then we'd have to try to carry him."

"I could call Sir Richard—or even Mr. Webster or—or the American—"

"Unbelievers," Lady Mary declared. "They'd only send out negative impulses and then we couldn't make contact at all. No—no—just you and I, Kate—and hurry, there's a good girl. Carry the candle—bring your matches—"

She could only obey and she put on her little white fur slippers and followed Lady Mary into the passage, through the great hall and down then into the cellars. There Lady Mary paused to open a high old wooden cabinet in which hung hundreds of keys. She chose a huge key of bronze, green with age, and with it opened a narrow door that led into a winding corridor.

"My lady," Kate, silent until now, spoke anxiously. "Are you sure you won't catch cold? It's been ages since anybody was down here—the air is like death itself."

"There's no such thing as death, not really," Lady Mary said. "It's just a change to something—I've told you—another level of whatever it is that we call life. It's only a transfer of energy. Can you understand? Please try, Kate! It would mean so much to me if someone did."

Lady Mary paused in the dim corridor. Her face was beautifully alive now, her eyes tender, her voice warm. Kate felt a deep longing to believe in her, and at the same time an impulse to run away, to fly back to the great hall, to find someone young and untouched by strangeness, someone like herself. Yet who was young in the castle except John Blayne? And he was still a stranger, someone from a new world.

"It's like the wireless, I tell you," Lady Mary was saying. "There's an instrument of transmission in us, but not everyone understands how to use it. Some day we'll know quite easily and then nobody will think it strange or talk about ghosts. It's only because we don't quite know yet—or so few of us do—"

The dreadful thought crossed Kate's mind now that Lady Mary might be going mad. She lifted the candle involuntarily so that the light fell on her face. Lady Mary stepped back. "Don't do that," she cried. "It hurts me."

She is going mad, Kate thought desperately, and tears came welling into her eyes. Through their shimmering she saw, or thought she saw, a nimbus about Lady Mary's head, like that of madonnas in old paintings.

She set the candle on a deep windowsill and put her arms about Lady Mary. "You aren't well, dear," she said. "You look so strangely at me. Perhaps you're only tired with all the anxiety—it would be natural."

Lady Mary drew back gently but firmly. "Stop shivering, child. I am not going mad and I feel quite clearly what you're thinking. There's nothing strange—it's all quite common sense, but I won't go into it now. Remember what we're here for—it's to ask *them* to show us treasure, if there is any."

She turned away from Kate and walked ahead of her down a long winding passage that descended almost imperceptibly as they went. She walked as if she were asleep, purposefully, familiarly, her step sure, her bearing confident. She was talking, not to herself exactly, Kate thought, and certainly not to her, but as if to someone who was walking just ahead. "We need a million dollars. That's what the American offers us. How much is that in pounds? Yes, it's a great many pounds—at any rate, more than we could possibly get together, and Government won't do anything. And not just rubies in the tennis court, please—this is serious. It's the castle now, the whole castle, and where are we to go if it's taken from us? Where are *you* to go?"

Kate was melted into pity and fresh alarm. "Ah now, Lady Mary dear, let's go back and find somebody!"

"Nonsense," Lady Mary said firmly. "We're going straight ahead. *They'll* speak when *they* can."

And she led the way down to the dungeons.

. . . Sir Richard opened his eyes and stared about the room. It was still dark, the intense darkness before dawn. A voice echoed in his ears, a woman's voice.

"Who's there?" he shouted.

No one answered. He thought nevertheless that he heard breathing, a fluttering sort of breath, a rustle somewhere near the northern window. He fumbled on the table for his matches and knocked the box to the floor.

"Damn," he said in a loud voice. He switched on the bedside lamp, knowing he must find the matches in case he had need of the candle. He got out of bed and knelt on the stone floor in his old-fashioned nightshirt, his bare knees chilled, and felt as far as he could reach. No matchbox!

"Damn, damn," he muttered between clenched teeth. He got to his feet stiffly and kicked about until he found his slippers, then shuffled over to the window, knocking his leg on a corner of his desk. The shuttered window was open and the light of a sinking moon shone palely over the yew walk and the lawn. The elephants loomed monstrously large, their shadows black. He could see nothing else and he leaned out and called.

"You there—speak up!"

No one spoke, but a flock of birds sleeping in the ivy flew out in alarm. He chuckled.

"It was you then, you rascals!" For a moment he stood by the window breathing in the good air that had been so recently washed with rain, then he yawned and shuffled back to the bed, stumbling over the elusive matchbox on the way. He got in, pulled the covers about him, and tried to sleep again. It was impossible. The events of the past two days came alive in his mind and he lived over each detail. This American! He envied the youth, the gaiety, the confident power of the man. A foreboding fell upon him. Again and again England had been revived by youth of other lands. Here in his own castle, built upon Roman foundations, young Danes, coming from France as conquerors, had created a strong new life. He switched on the lamp by his bed and reached for a book he had been reading.

"Oh France," the ancient chronicler declared, "Thou layest stricken and low upon the ground . . . But, behold, from Denmark came forth a new race . . . Compact was made, between her and thee. This race will lift up thy name and dominion to the skies."

"And how great the blend had been," the book said, "old Roman order with youthful human energy!"

He sighed, and knew he could not sleep. Was he not now of the old order? And did John Blayne indeed bring in the new? He laid the book away and put out the light. Shivering, he drew up the covers and fell into a troubled sleep, distressed by clouded dreams.

Hours later, or perhaps only minutes, he was wakened, or dreamed he was wakened, by the deep vague melancholy that he had come to know so well, preceding always the restless, throbbing pain inside his skull. Here it was again—and how to escape it? He dreaded the darkness that fell upon his mind. Light! He must find light. Where was the light? He could not breathe, he struggled to open his eyes, and then as if he were in heavy chains, he got slowly out of bed, fumbling for the light and unable to find it, then fumbling for the matches but he could not put his hand on the box.

He remembered that behind the swinging panel he kept matches and a candle, and he groped his way to the wall. He felt for the particular spot, the center of a star in the carving of the panel. He pressed it. The wall, which no one knew was a door except himself and Wells, swung creaking away from him. He went through it and closed it again carefully. Then he felt along the wall and found the alcove and the matchbox. The first three matches would not strike for dampness but he fumbled for the bottom match and then the flame held. He lit the candle and, blind with pain, he walked down the passage to the winding stair at its end and still with a strange purposefulness, as though he were deep in sleep, he climbed to the top, two flights up to the east tower. There the passage narrowed until it barely admitted his lean figure. At the end a door filled its width, an arched door, very low. He opened it and entered an octagonal room.

The light of the candle fell upon the thin figure of Wells, his hair in disarray and dusty with cobwebs.

He dropped on one knee. "Good evening, Your Majesty. I'd about given you up."

Sir Richard put out his hand. Wells kissed it.

"Rise, Lord Dunsten," Sir Richard said.

Wells rose, bowed deeply, and then as though it were a ritual long established, he took the candle from Sir Richard and set it on the table.

"Pray be seated, Your Majesty," he said.

With these words, he pulled back from the table a massive oak chair. It was covered with a tattered robe of purple velvet, and this he wrapped about Sir Richard, who seated himself and waited in solemn silence while Wells went to a long narrow chest, also of oak, that stood against the wall. This chest he opened, lifting the heavy lid with effort and leaning it against the wall. From the chest he took out a large leather-bound book, fastened by silver hasps. He carried it to the table in both hands and set it before Sir Richard, who sat unmoving, his gaze downcast. Then, returning to the chest, Wells lifted from it a large scepter of heavy gold encrusted with jewels. This he carried, again in both hands, to Sir Richard, who took it in his right hand. Once more Wells went to the chest and now he took from it a crown of gold tinsel, cut into five high points, each point with a star of silver paste. This crown he took and set on Sir Richard's head.

Then he bowed again deeply. "Is there anything else, Your Majesty?" he asked.

"Nothing, Lord Dunsten," Sir Richard replied. "You may retire."

"Thank you, Your Majesty," Wells said.

He had backed only a few steps toward the door, however, when Sir Richard lifted his left hand to stop him.

"One question, Lord Dunsten."

"Yes, Your Majesty?"

"As my faithful prime minister, have you put down the plot to rob me of my crown?"

"You have nothing to fear, Your Majesty," Wells said. He waited for what Sir Richard might say next, a look of anxious concern upon his long lean face, the shadows dark in his sunken cheeks.

Sir Richard sighed a deep and heartbreaking sigh. "Ah, my enemies seek my end! They will put an end to all kings—you'll see—you'll see! They will kill Richard the Fourth as they killed other kings."

"No one knows you are here, Your Majesty."

"No one but you," Sir Richard said.

Wells bowed. "We are well hidden and I will never betray you, Sire."

Sir Richard turned his nobly shaped head, gave Wells a royal look, and held out his right hand. On the forefinger was the gold ring set with the large ruby. Wells came forward and bowing over it, he kissed it.

Sir Richard spoke with touching dignity.

"You deserve to be Lord Protector—I'll make you that, one day. I know how to reward your loyalty—what you did for me once, long ago—"

"Please, Your Majesty," Wells broke in. He wrung his long thin hands. "We agreed that it was never to be brought up. The boy is dead."

Sir Richard corrected him. "The Prince is dead—and I never—never—forget."

His chin sank upon his breast for an instant and his eyes closed. The pain, the pain! He struggled against losing himself. He was sinking into darkness, into death, alive only to pain. He made great effort and felt himself rising up again. Suddenly he gave a start, lifted his head, drew the candlestick near, opened the book and began to read. Wells watched him for a moment, then backed silently to the door. There he stood for yet another moment. The candlelight fell upon the figure in the purple robe, upon the handsome aging profile, upon the crown and scepter, and upon the high back of the chair.

It was a throne.

. . . Deep in the dungeon beneath the castle a sound reverberated with an echoing roar. Kate looked up, alarmed, her hand shielding the candle.

"What's that, my lady?"

Lady Mary continued her careful search of the crannied wall. "A door banging," she said absently.

"It sounded like the lid of a coffin," Kate said.

"Nonsense," Lady Mary retorted. She found a stone loose, a small stone in a crack between two large blocks and she worked it free and peered inside. "There's something here," she exclaimed. She felt inside the aperture and brought out a crooked spoon of silver, green with age.

"Nothing else," she said. "Some poor prisoner, I suppose, hiding his spoon so that he needn't eat with his fingers."

Far above their heads they heard now a sudden clatter of metal. Kate cried out, "My lady, don't tell me that sounds like nothing!"

Lady Mary listened. "It sounds like gold pieces," she exclaimed. Her face lighted with excitement, and lifting her head she called.

'Whoever you are, wherever you are—where do I go?"

They listened, waiting, motionless, Kate believing, almost, that Lady Mary would be given an answer. But there was none. The silence deepened and suddenly the air in the dungeon that was thick with mildew and dust seemed too heavy to breathe. Kate, borne up by excitement until now, was suddenly depressed and frightened. She looked at Lady Mary. Her face was ashen and her blue eyes had faded in the candlelight to a pale gray.

"My lady," Kate cried, "we must go back! The air is deathly here—poisonous, my lady! We'll be suffocated— Ah now, don't faint! What did I tell you?"

Lady Mary did indeed seem on the edge of fainting away. She leaned on Kate's shoulder, gasping for breath.

"Let me open that door yonder," Kate cried and with one arm supporting Lady Mary and the other holding the candle, she led the way to a door opposite the stairway and, setting the candle on a jutting ledge of rough rock, she tried to force the door open. It would not open, however she pushed against it. The latch was old and rusted and did not yield.

"There's nothing for it," she declared swiftly. "We'll have to go up the stair again. Cling to me, my lady, we'll make it somehow. . . . This way, dear. The stones are smoother here, where some poor prisoner paced back and forth perhaps until he died. . . . I blame myself that I let you come here at all. I should have known better."

Painfully they climbed the stone steps until they were at the top. A stone ledge stood under a window so high and narrow that it was no more than a gash in the wall.

"Sit down for a bit, my lady," Kate said. "I'll run for my grandfather to help us. . . . Dare I leave you?"

"I shall be quite all right," Lady Mary said faintly but with resolution.

"And I'll be back immediately," Kate said, "and then you must get in bed again and have a cup of nice hot tea."

She kissed Lady Mary's cheek impulsively and ran through the corridors and passages to her grandfather's room.

Left alone Lady Mary continued to sit on the stone ledge in the wall. She clasped her hands on her lap, not together, but one hand laid in the other, palm up, like a bowl, waiting to receive. She gathered her strength, closed her eyes, and concentrated on the familiar long dark tunnel and upon the silver spot of light at its end.

"I give myself up," she said in a low clear voice. "I am empty. I am waiting—waiting—waiting—"

She lifted her head to listen, she opened her eyes. There was a voice—yes, distinctly there was a voice—no, two voices, somewhere far above her. To the left? No, the right—difficult to tell! They echoed strangely beyond and above and—everywhere. She could not hear the words— not quite. Then she heard almost clearly—"Your Majesty—" She felt suddenly faint. Then it was true. She had not only imagined. It was more than the wind in the ivy clinging to the walls. Others did live here in the castle.

Her head drooped upon her breast. Her hands grew limp and her eyes closed.

. . . "Grandfather!" Kate called.

There was no answer. She flung open the door. The room was dim in the approaching dawn. She entered and looked behind the curtains at the old-fashioned bed where Wells slept. He was not there.

"Whatever!" Kate muttered to herself. "He can't have gone to the kitchens so early as this."

She ran out of the room again and had scarcely gone twenty feet when she heard a loud shout from the direction of the Duke's room. The bell rang violently and she heard a door flung open.

"What the devil!" John Blayne roared.

"Wait," she cried. "I'm coming."

She made haste in the direction of the Duke's room. John stood there in the doorway. She put back her hair and tied the sash of her dressing gown more tightly about her waist.

"What is it, please?" she asked, and could not but

notice how his crimson satin dressing gown became him, and how young he looked, his hair every which way and his face fresh with sleep.

He tried to laugh. "Idiotic—but I saw a sort of floating head going by the window! Somebody is playing jokes."

"You were dreaming," she said.

He rubbed his hands through his hair and lifted his eyebrows. "Dreaming? Maybe I am. Where did you come from, for example?"

"I am looking for my grandfather. Have you see him?"

"At this hour? No. . . . Is something wrong?"

"I don't know."

"What do you mean? You don't know? Is someone ill?"

"I don't think so but—"

"You're ill!"

He stepped forward and put his hands on her shoulders. "You're shivering—yes, you are! Why are you wandering about at this time of night if you aren't ill? Or frightened?"

He had her hands now and was chafing them.

"Perhaps I am frightened—a little," she confessed.

"Which I can fully understand," he went on, "for I'll confess now, to you, that at this hour of the night your castle gives me the creeps. I don't believe a word of what Lady Mary says, mind you—but I have the creeps, nevertheless. I don't believe I saw a head without a body floating past my window, but I did. How in the devil have you lived here all your life and stayed what you are?"

She was smiling into his eyes, drinking in what he was saying. "How do you know what I am? You never saw me until yesterday!"

"I know a rose when I see one," he said, half teasing. "And a rose by any other name than yours is not as sweet, Shakespeare notwithstanding."

She was trembling now and not with cold. She must stop this at once, this impossible talk, this—this absurd way she felt—this melting and dissolving inside herself.

"Oh," she cried softly, "what am I doing? I've forgotten Lady Mary!"

She pulled her hands away and fled.

. . . She disappeared so quickly that he could almost have believed that she sank through the floor except that it was stone, or slid through an unseen door, except that there was no door. The winding corridors hid her instantly, but he ran after her nevertheless, and found himself in a tangle of passages. It was no use. He could not find her and wandering indefinitely in the dim light before dawn, he could only be lost in the end. Indeed he was already lost. Which was his door? He had left it ajar but a strange cold wind blew through the corridors and no doors were open.

"What the devil is going on?" he muttered as he went this way and that.

And speaking of devils, he thought, where was Wells? He was reminded of the fellow now by a long, frayed bell rope that hung meaninglessly against a wall. He pulled it and heard a distant high jangle, but no one came. He pulled again, this time with force, and the velvet rope fell from the groined ceiling and wound about his shoulders like a snake. He threw it on the floor in disgust. There was nothing for it but to find his way back by wandering. There must be an end somewhere to this corridor.

He walked for several minutes, then the corridor made a sharp right-angle turn. He paused and looked straight ahead for fifty feet or more. The passage was windowless but at the end he saw a tall motionless figure, vague in the darkness.

"Wells!"

There was no answer. The man stood motionless. He went forward uncertainly until he was near enough to put out his hand. He felt cold steel. The man was a coat of armor—no more, no less! He burst into laughter and at himself.

"I am getting as crazy as you are, my good man," he muttered. His voice echoed strangely between the stone walls and he tried to laugh again and found he could not.

"An empty shell of a man, that's what you are," he said loudly, "and that's what we'll all be if we stay here much longer." He turned and strode back in the direction in which he had come.

He had not gone far, however, when he heard a low deep groan that ended in a choking gasp. He stopped. The noise came from behind a door some twenty feet ahead of him. He went to it and knocked. No one replied. He tried the door softly and it opened. A candle burned on a table beside a heavily curtained bed. From behind the curtains the groan broke forth again, ending in the choking gurgling gasp. He tiptoed across the floor and drew aside the worn red satin curtains. There under a tattered silken coverlet Webster lay sleeping, flat upon his back, his rough beard upthrust. The groan and gurgle gathered in his throat again, ready to explode.

He drew the curtains hastily together upon the hideous sight. Let Webster sleep, if he could—if anyone could in this ghostly dwelling place! He would get back to his own room somehow although he might be more lost than he imagined, in this Jules Verne sort of bewilderment, a relapse of time, a confusion of centuries. Though why Jules Verne, when Einstein himself in this modern age had declared the eternity of time? History repeating itself was a truism, simple enough until Einstein made his portentous discoveries. What if time were indeed a circle, a never-ending merry-go-round, repeating again and again the identical? What if all this were merely a remnant of time, a sort of neutrino, an ash of what had happened long ago?

Stop it, he said to himself. Get hold of yourself, stop these antics of your brain! This was the sort of thinking a brain did at night when the conscious will was sleeping at the controls. Nightmares!

He broke off his self-admonishment. He saw beneath his feet a broad white line encircling Webster's bed. He took up the candle and followed it. It was a line drawn unevenly upon the ancient floor, a chalk line, marked here and there by crude crosses. He walked its length and then returned to put the candle on the table. A chalk line —and crosses! Where had he heard that ancient superstition? In Ireland, of course, in the last summer of his mother's life! She had wanted to see the green isle again and he had taken her to County Wicklow and they had spent a fortnight there, walking over the dark hills and picnicking beside a deep tarn in some lovely valley. A farmer's wife had told him one night in a thatched-roofed farmhouse where he and his mother had taken shelter in a sudden storm, that though spirits walked the hillside and even came into the house, "they can't touch you, sir, if you'll but draw a white chalk line around the bed you sleep on, and put in plenty of crosses."

So Webster was Irish! Ah yes, that explained it, and what was this on the table? A bottle of water blessed by some priest, no doubt, and therefore holy. The floor was patterned dustily with stains of the water—yes, and here was a Bible and upon it, cautious man, this Webster had placed a small pearl-handled pistol of ancient design, a relic, doubtless, that he had found somewhere in the castle and had appropriated for the night.

He smiled grimly to himself. Brave Webster, pretending a mighty courage when he was with others, a high skepticism, but when alone, resorting to most ancient protection! He lifted the silver snuffer on the table and extinguished the candle. Then he felt his way to the door. When he tried to close it softly, however, one of those

gusts of unexplained wind snatched it from his grasp.
It slammed shut with an ear-cracking bang. He heard a
loud yell from within. Webster had wakened. He opened
the door again to explain and was met by a splash of
cold water in his face. He gasped and stepped back.

"Webster!" he shouted. "What are you doing? It's I—
John Blayne!"

"Heaven save us—" he heard Webster mutter. A match
was struck and a moment later the candle flared. Webster
stood by the bed, staring at him.

"What are you doing here, man—at this time of the
night?"

"It's not night any more," he retorted. "It's near dawn,
as you would see if you hadn't sealed yourself with chalk
marks and Bibles and pistols and so on—not to mention
this bath of water you've dashed in my face!"

"Holy water never hurt anyone," Webster retorted,
"and if you can stop laughing, tell me why you are up
and wandering about the castle? I'm sure you don't get
up at dawn any more than I do."

"I had a nightmare, if you must know the truth," John
Blayne said. He was wiping the water from his face and
neck with his handkerchief.

"A nightmare, was it?" Webster repeated.

"Nothing but a nightmare—a head, if you please,
swimming past my window with no body attached. Now
don't indulge yourself in delightful fancies! There's a
terrace outside my window, I daresay, and someone—
Wells, doubtless, who's desiccated enough to look like an
authentic ghost anywhere, not mentioning in this castle
—was probably taking a midnight walk."

"I'm going back to bed," Webster said. "I get a chill
easily at my age."

John Blayne was amused. "Really? And I was about
to ask you to go with me to my room to investigate the
head, just for the sake of finding out facts. I'm a great

believer in facts. If you're afraid, now that you've wasted all of the holy water on me, you could carry the Bible in one hand and the pistol in the other."

"I'm afraid of nobody," Webster shouted, "and it's cold that makes my teeth chatter, nothing else!"

"Come along then, but it's a distance, I warn you. I've been lost for hours."

"Nonsense," Webster said sourly. "Your room isn't minutes down the passage from mine."

He took Webster's arm and led the way in long strides, Webster guiding him, to the Duke's room.

"Lucky I found you," he said, as they walked. "I swear I've been searching for my room for the past hour and a half. Now you tell me it's two minutes away, no more. Ah yes—right you are! I remember the coat of arms carved on the door—a handsome door, by the way, heavy as—"

He heaved at the door as he spoke, but it opened easily as though someone pulled it from within and they all but fell into the room. Wells stood there, tall and correct even in his nightclothes.

"Mr. Blayne," he exclaimed. "Where have you been? I've been looking for you everywhere. I thought I heard you call."

John Blayne stared at him. "Did you walk past my window on the terrace?"

"What terrace, sir?"

"Don't make a joke, Wells! I like jokes, mind you, but not heads without bodies floating past my window!"

He spoke lightly and was astonished at the change that suddenly took place in the old man. Wells set his jaws tight. His eyes narrowed in their piercing gaze, his gray and brushy eyebrows knit over his long nose.

"How dare you, making jokes about the Duke of Starborough's head!"

John Blayne surprised, stepped back, but Wells stepped

toward him and spoke between clenched teeth, "If you knew who I am, you wouldn't dare—you wouldn't dare!"

Staring, John Blayne felt just then that he knew all too well who Wells was—Kate's grandfather, the indispensable butler, but what had that to do with the Duke's head and an imagined insult? "Really, Wells," he began, "I'm sorry, but . . ."

Walking past him with eyes that deigned not to countenance him, Wells went to the door, opened it, and disappeared down the passage.

"Is the man mad?" John Blayne asked.

He was amazed to see only embarrassment on Webster's face, not fright or concern, when he answered, "Not mad, odd perhaps. Yes, I'll agree that he's odd. He does some playacting now and then as does the old boy himself. I think it goes to his head a bit."

"Sir Richard? Playacting?"

"Yes, I regret to say," Webster sighed. "There are some odd situations here, I admit, more than can be told."

"Who is Wells?" John Blayne demanded. "Or who does he think he is?"

"He—he's the butler," Webster said uncertainly.

John Blayne stared at him. "I don't believe it."

Webster coughed. "Why not?"

"I'll ask another question, too." He stepped forward and tapped Webster's chest. "Who is Kate?"

Webster stepped back. "Kate? Just what you see, an uncommonly attractive young woman, of course. She makes herself useful in several ways—here in the castle the maid, and so forth—"

He interrupted. "She is not only attractive, she's lovely. A maid? What maid is treated like Kate? She's like a daughter to the family, and—"

Webster broke in. "Nonsense! They sit, she stands. She doesn't take her meals in the great hall with Lady Mary

and Sir Richard. It's true that she—but in England a
child is taught to call her father 'sir'—"

John Blayne caught him up sharply. "Father? Who?"

"I thought you meant Sir Richard."

"Sir Richard!"

Webster recovered himself. "I really don't know what
you are talking about, Blayne. In fact, I really don't know
why I'm here. Some joke or other, and I don't care for
jokes at this time of night—or day—whatever—If you'll
excuse me—"

John Blayne felt an explosion of anger in his head.
"You will excuse me," he said. "It's I who am leaving.
I shall drop this whole project. It is no longer attractive
to me. If you will be so kind as to tell Sir Richard in
the morning that I have left—"

He felt Webster's grip on his shoulder.

"You can't simply leave—not at this point. You have
gone too far. We can sue you—"

He wrestled himself free. "Sue me, by all means! I'll
notify my lawyers. And if you will please leave—my
room."

He waited but Webster did not leave. Instead he tied
the belt of his brown flannel dressing gown more firmly
about his wide waist, then strolled across the room and
sat down in a huge old crimson velvet chair. He made
a pretense of laughter.

"Come now, Blayne—you'll have me believing that
you're afraid of ghosts yourself, and that's why you don't
want the castle."

He refused the laughter. "You know very well I'm
afraid of nothing. It's simply that I can't trust anyone
here. At dinner you declare that Lady Mary is talking
nonsense—but what do I discover in the middle of the
night? You—and all those barbaric tricks! You're a liar,
Webster."

Webster leaped to his feet. "A liar, am I? Did you

see a head or didn't you? Tell me that—just yes or no—"

"Yes."

"You had no business to barge into my room—"

They faced each other like two angry cocks. He stared into Webster's bulbous gray eyes. In the half light of the dawn he saw what an absurd face Webster's was, with its pudgy nose, tight little mouth, and ragged beard. He burst out laughing suddenly and put out his hand.

"Sit down again," he commanded. "I'm not going to let you off now that I've got you in my power. I'm simply eaten up with vulgar curiosity. Tell me—"

Hands on Webster's shoulders, he pressed him into the big chair and then drew up a hassock whose yellow satin cover was almost in shreds.

"Tell me honestly, confidentially, fully—any way you like—who is Wells and who is Kate? I smell a secret—very dusty and moldy like everything else here in the castle. Perhaps it needs sun and air, too. . . . Come, don't pretend with me, Webster! We're not children, in spite of all this hocus-pocus!"

Webster shivered slightly. "It's damp—very dangerous! My toes are curling up!" He pulled up his collar and thrust his hands into the pockets of his dressing gown.

"All right, Mr. Webster. Begin!" he said firmly.

Webster sneezed long and loudly, blew his nose, glanced at him and away again and had a fit of coughing before he could answer.

"Yes, well—let me see—in answer to your question—about Wells, wasn't it? He's quite what he looks, you know. He was a young footman here when Sir Richard was born, and gradually rose to be the butler. He married a farmer's daughter named Elsie—very pretty girl, I remember, much younger than himself—and she died in giving birth to their only son, Colin. He was Kate's father, of course—a very troublesome lad."

"Explain 'troublesome'!"

Webster coughed again. "I'll catch my death here if I don't look out. . . . Troublesome? Well, restless, you know—always a bit above his station. He was a bright child, and Sir Richard spoiled him—a handsome boy—looked like his Irish mother. Pity that Richard had no children of his own!"

"Whose fault?"

Webster lifted his eyebrows. "Fault? I shouldn't call it that, exactly. Nobody's, really. It happens sometimes that two people can't have children together for some occult psychological reason, but are quite able if it's with someone else—Ah, but that's neither here nor there! Sir Richard has always been devoted to his wife. No, no—it was quite natural for him to be amused by Colin. The boy had a frank fearless way with him and followed Sir Richard about—learning to ride well, and so on—developed quite a talent in painting too. Sir Richard sent him to a school. Wells disapproved of all that spoiling, I remember. He said it put the boy above his station."

"But Sir Richard persisted?"

"Well, in a way I suppose he was right. The boy was somehow—unusual, let's say. It was difficult for visitors to believe he was only the butler's son, you know."

"How did they have a chance to see him?"

"Well . . ." Webster hesitated.

"Come, man," John Blayne said impatiently. "I'm not pulling your teeth, you know!"

"Well, Sir Richard would have him in, you know, at teatime or after dinner, show him off, let him recite poems and so on."

"In spite of Wells' protests?"

"Yes, I suppose so. The boy was a superior sort, obviously. And devoted to Sir Richard as a consequence of the spoiling."

"Sir Richard couldn't bear to see Colin a servant?" He put the question sharply.

Webster considered. "As to that, Colin could not bear to see himself a servant."

"So, he ran away to London, became an artist, then the war gave him the chance to become a hero. He married, as you so quaintly like to say it 'above his position' and—" John Blayne got up from the hassock and walked across the room and back again. "I'm beginning to understand."

"Who told you that part of the story?"

"Never mind, I just got the end before the beginning. It's true, isn't it?"

Webster shrugged his shoulders. "Oh yes, as true as anything is in life."

"What's true is true, you're a lawyer and you should know that."

Again Webster shrugged his shoulders, then hunched himself further into the chair in search of warmth.

"Why did Lady Mary consent to all this?"

"Why shouldn't she?" Webster bristled as if beginning defense of a client. "Sir Richard and Lady Mary are two very kind and wonderful people. I'm sure they longed for children of their own. Certainly Sir Richard has grieved because there's no heir."

"I wonder how a man feels when it's his fault he has no child."

Now it was Webster who got up and paced the floor. "Really, Mr. Blayne, I don't know how we got on the subject. I—well, let me say that I know it wasn't Sir Richard's fault, as you put it—though I repudiate the word."

"Was there never talk of a divorce?"

"Of course not! He wouldn't want to hurt his wife, even though he has no heir! Do you take him for the Shah of Persia? Only kings *have* to produce offspring!"

He was relentless. "You mean there *is* a child some-where?"

Webster shouted. "No—no—no! I mean no such thing. . . . Besides, he's far too old—"

He broke in. "You know very well, Webster—you ought to know—if there is a child we'll have a problem. He would be the heir to the castle."

They faced each other again.

"There is no heir," Webster said at last. "And I'll thank you to let me go back to bed."

"Of course."

He opened the door with obvious patience, and when Webster had walked through in silence he closed it and stood thinking, his hands in the pockets of his dressing gown.

No heir, Webster had said. No son, that was, but per-haps a child? And the child could be—Kate? Ah, but a link was missing, an essential link. Who—who was Colin? He was not leaving the castle—not yet!

. . . "Lady Mary!" Kate called. She had escaped safely again. Ah, but it was dangerous, meeting John Blayne like that, Kate thought, the two of them alone, and he reaching out for her, and her blood going into a turmoil at his touch. She'd never been quite in love although once, long ago, there had been a boy in the village, but Sir Richard had put an end to that. She could remember the moment as clear as yesterday, for she had never seen him so angry. He had stopped her in the great hall, alone.

"You will remember who you are," he had said and had drawn down his eyebrows until his eyes were hidden. "I will not have the son of a farmer here in my castle."

"I wasn't—I didn't dream of him coming here," she had faltered.

"Even more disgraceful for you to meet him in secret," he had said. "You'll never see him again. I forbid it."

She had run away, she was so frightened. And the boy's family had been dismissed from the farm. She had a penciled letter on a bit of paper from the boy. "I am far away Katie not seeing you no more." She had been repelled by the ill-written message and had soon forgotten him, but not, she knew, the excitement. Ah, Sir Richard would be just as angry if he knew now!

And then she saw Lady Mary, waiting where she had been left, in the stone corridor to the dungeon and she ran to her. Lady Mary did not move. She sat with her hands palms up on her lap, her eyes half closed.

"Wake up, my dear! . . . I'm back. Everything is quite all right. . . . And it's nearly morning."

She was rubbing Lady Mary's cold hands as she spoke. She smoothed back Lady Mary's silvery hair. There was no answer from the still figure, sitting on the damp stone ledge, her head drooping on her breast.

"God save us," Kate whispered in sudden terror. "Have *they* killed her for wanting help from *them?* . . . Lady Mary, can you hear me, darling?"

Lady Mary did not answer, but Kate knew that she could hear.

"Help me," Kate whispered, looking about her. "I'll have to carry her somehow."

She put her arm under Lady Mary's shoulder and supported her as she walked.

"Ah, me," she said under her breath. "She's so light— no more than a ghost herself. Oh, this wicked old castle —oh dear, oh dear—I wish—indeed I wish—"

And sighing and fearful, she helped Lady Mary back to her room and laid her on the bed.

. . . At breakfast the next morning Wells was his usual imperturbable self as he presided over the serving dishes

on the buffet. Sir Richard sat with remote but kingly
mien at his end of the table. Philip Webster was chipper
as ever. Lady Mary was not in her usual place as she
was being served by Kate in her bedroom.

The sun was streaming brilliantly into the great hall,
its bright beams falling on gray stone floors and tapestried
walls. Windows were wide open and even the door that
led out to the garden. Spring air sweet and fresh was
flowing through the castle. John Blayne had begun to
wonder if the previous night's experiences had been
dreams, after all. But no, he reminded himself, he had
been given fragments of a story that had taken place
within these very walls, a story that might be as mean-
ingful to him as ancient events were to Sir Richard and
Lady Mary.

"Mr. Blayne," Sir Richard had said when they first met
at the breakfast table, "I have been endeavoring to decide
what will be the best thing for me to do for my realm—
my tenants, that is. Until my decision is clear, you may
call in your young men and proceed with the measurements you wish to have made."

"I'm certainly glad to have something for them to do,
Sir Richard. They've been fretting a bit down at the inn."

"Better be busy, even if it comes to nothing, than drink
ale all day and listen to gossip," Sir Richard said.

A quick series of telephone calls was made and before
an hour had passed, the rooms of the castle were alive
with the four young men busily coming and going. With
coats off, sleeves rolled up and collars loosened, they
moved about their tasks efficiently and excitedly. Now
they were men with a purpose, men with pencils and papers, huge sheets of paper, foot rules, tapes, and blueprint
maps. A surveyor squinted through his telescope and
checked against a measuring line. A draughtsman recorded
his finding in a large notebook. Among them moved John
Blayne with calm assurance and brisk commands. He was

cheerful and resolute, his chin outthrust, his dark eyes alert. The absurdities of the night were past.

"The glass panes must be counted, numbered to each window, the window to each room, against the time when they'll be packed in cotton. We'd never be able to duplicate that glass."

"We're going full steam ahead, whatever the decision is," he said to his men. "If we have to stop, we'll stop. If not, then we'll be that much ahead. I'm paying you, don't forget! Well, then, on with the job."

He was enjoying himself, that was obvious. Nothing suited him better than carrying on some huge enterprise with a purpose, and the purpose now was enhanced by the mystery of Kate. He kept watch for her but she had not yet appeared. Five more minutes and he would go in search. He took off his coat and tie, and the morning wind rumpled his hair and sent stinging red blood to his cheeks. He had never felt better and he shouted his orders and interlarded them with jokes.

"If you find one of those ghosts they are always talking about, attach a note to him as to where he belongs. We'll put him back in his hole again if he gets to Connecticut. Keep them all happy, that's what I say, even the ghosts. . . . If she's a queen, let me have a look at her first! . . . Easy there, Johnston! These mullioned panes of glass aren't meant to look through—they're valued as diamonds."

In the midst of the banter and the bustle he heard a small scream from the swinging doors into the great hall. He looked up and saw Kate, her hands pressed over her mouth.

"Come in," he called. "Come in, Rose of the morning!"

She advanced on him slowly, looking very pretty, he noticed, in a blue linen dress and a little ruffled white apron.

"What on earth are you doing?" she demanded.

"Whatever you see," he replied with an easy smile.

"What I see," she said distinctly, "whatever it is, all of it, has got to stop—this instant!"

He squinted an eye along a ruler he held up to a window. "Now why," he said pleasantly, "why do you shout at me when you know that I hear the slightest sound, the creeping footsteps of a mouse, the rustle of a bird's wing, the whisper of a girl's voice, the whimper of a ghost—"

She stopped his nonsense by stamping her foot. "Tell your men to clear out of the castle!"

"When I'm paying them handsome dollars to work here? Come now—" He scribbled some figures on a sheet of paper on the table.

"If you don't, I will," she declared.

He smiled and went on writing and she clapped her hands. The men stopped what they were doing to look at her.

"Men!" Her clear flutelike voice rang through the spaces. "Will you kindly leave at once?"

"Do we go?" One of them turned to John Blayne.

He did not look up. He was adding the figures down a long column and waited until he had the total. "Certainly not," he said then. "I have given orders, haven't I?"

The men went on with their work.

Out of the corner of his eye John Blayne saw Kate approach him. She came to his side and spoke into his right ear. "I shall go to Sir Richard this instant."

He replied in pretended absence of mind, his mind on figures, it appeared, and his every sense aware of her, the fragrance, the beauty. "Why didn't you go to him in the first place?" he said calmly. "Always go to the top, is what I advise. No use jumping on me—I don't own the castle, you know."

She tapped his shoulder with her forefinger. "You'll come with me, please!"

He straightened and looked at her, innocence in his eyes. "Why should I? I'm not stealing the castle, either. I'm not even behaving as though I meant to—I'm just keeping my men busy. Whatever I'm doing, it's all cleared with Webster. I'm within my rights."

His look, so gay, so impudent, was unbearable. She opened her mouth and closed it, unable for the instant to say a word and then began to stammer, "You—you—I'll—I'll have you know—I'll show you—I'll—"

"Take it easy, little Kate," he said.

She gave up, stifled by fury, and while he laughed at her, she ran like a child across the room and into a great hall in the direction of Sir Richard's library and knocked on the door. There was no answer. She laid her ear against the oak panel and listened, then opened the door. He was not there.

She ran down the passageway to his bedroom. He might still be asleep—it had been such an odd night, with everyone awake at some time or other. She threw open the door of his bedroom. He was not there. Where was Wells? He would know—and now she ran to the kitchens and the pantry to find him. The two of them must be gone somewhere. Sometimes they did go wandering about like two old hounds— No one knew where. But Wells was not to be found, either. There was nothing then to do but to go to Lady Mary.

She tiptoed to the door and opened it. Lady Mary was still resting in her bed. Under the canopy of faded rose silk she lay upon her piled pillows, her delicate profile clear, the white hair flowing back from her pale face, a film of lace upon her head and her hands folded on her breast. At the sound of the door opening on its heavy hinges she opened her eyes and sat up.

Kate ran to the bedside. "Lady Mary, dear! Whatever

is it? You're pale as a ghost. What have you seen now!"

"Why did you wake me?"

Her voice was strangely sad, and Kate was put to confusion. "I was looking for Sir Richard, my lady. These Americans are taking over the castle. They're everywhere at once. I told him—"

"He?"

Kate took her listless hand. "Your hand's like ice, my lady. The American, John Blayne . . . I said, 'You must all leave at once.' He paid not the slightest heed, my lady, and so I told the men myself to leave but of course they didn't obey me and I was trying to find Sir Richard, but he's not to be found, and I ran here to tell you. You must speak to them, my lady—really you should—the way they're behaving as though—did you hear me, my lady?"

A strange gray glaze had come over Lady Mary's eyes. She sank back on her pillows and stared into the tattered canopy above her head.

"It would be best, perhaps," she muttered. "I'm not sure, after what I— It's not possible except that I did hear—quite clearly, you know, Kate, while you were so long gone, last night—I'm not imagining—or—or— dreaming or any of those things—two voices—no voice I'd ever heard—mumbling like an old, old man, 'They will kill Richard the Fourth . . . well hidden here'—and the other voice—oh, such an old trembling voice trying to be brave—'never betray you, Sire.' Sire! That's only for a king. What king, Kate?"

"I don't know, my lady," Kate faltered.

"You don't know," Lady Mary repeated slowly. "Nobody knows. But I heard those voices—sad, sad old voices —coming from far off somewhere in the walls, Kate. . . . *They* can hide in the walls, you know. *They* don't have bodies, poor things— Oh, do let's go away from this castle, Kate—or let the castle go away from us!"

She gazed at Kate in pleading, and Kate saw tears welling into the kind and piteous eyes. "Ah now, my lady," she said, coaxing. "You've been nightmaring, dear—it's all because of the old silly tales you've heard for so long. You don't feel well, that's what. I shall call the doctor—your head's hot and your hands are cold."

She took Lady Mary's thin wrist between her thumb and finger. "And your pulse, it's racing, my lady. Have you a chill?"

Lady Mary turned her face away on the pillow. "*They* can't help us, Kate, *they're* thinking only of *themselves*—remembering—that's all—remembering—remembering—Perhaps it's the only way *they* live now. There's only the past for *them*—no future. Of course there's no future—"

She's raving, Kate thought, or she's really seen something— Ah no, and nonsense! The room was oppressive and it seemed dark for such a fine day. She put down the slender hand she was still holding and went to the windows to draw the curtains farther back. The morning sun streamed through the ancient glass in broken prisms of color.

"It's such a day, my lady," she said cheerfully. "See the lovely sunshine! I do think the way it comes in colors through the glass is so pretty, don't you? I shall fetch some tea for you, and buttered toast. You'll feel better when you've had a little more to eat. It was a night, wasn't it! And today not much better—those Americans!"

She busied herself about the room as she talked, straightening the silver brushes on the toilet table, folding the silk dressing gown Lady Mary had dropped on the chaise longue, picking a leaf from the worn Aubusson carpet—the wind, doubtless, in the night—

"If you could see them, my lady," she went on, "climbing about the castle like—like mountain goats! I've never seen mountain goats, of course, but you'd laugh—really you would. Two of them are walking the battlements, measuring. I'd like to see them fall in the moat! They do take over, don't they? Americans are so beastly healthy—full of eggs and bacon, I daresay, and beefsteak, and those alphabetic vitamins they're always talking about! You shall have an egg for your breakfast this morning, my lamb. I left an order in the hen house yesterday. There's such a wise old hen there. An egg, if you please, I said, and she looked at me with one eye and then the other—and went to the nest at once, the darling."

She glanced at the bed as she talked. There was no sign that she was heard. Lady Mary lay staring into the canopy, motionless, her hand lying where it had dropped. Suddenly she gave a convulsive start. She sat up and looked at the east wall. Her hands flew to her cheeks and she moaned.

Kate ran to her side and poured water from the silver decanter into a tumbler. "Here, my lady—drink this! Yes, indeed, you must. Stop looking at the wall, my lady. . . . What do you see there? Tell me—tell me—"

She tried to pull her hands away, but Lady Mary was rigid. Kate put down the glass.

"I'll have to—I'll find Sir Richard, I'll be back in a minute, my lady, I promise."

Lady Mary neither spoke nor moved and Kate ran out of the room into the passage that led to Sir Richard's room. No use looking for him there—but she glanced into the open door nevertheless, and to her astonishment she saw him sitting now at the table by the open window. He was dressed in his usual tweeds, his hair neatly brushed, his face calm.

"Sir Richard!" she gasped. "Where did you come from? It was only a few minutes ago I was here."

He did not reply.

She came toward him. "Did you hear me call? You didn't answer—"

"You forget yourself, woman," he said sternly. "How dare you come into my room without permission?"

These were his words, spoken in cold, even hostile tones, and Kate could not believe what she heard. He looked so usual, so much himself, and yet this was certainly not he.

"I wanted to tell you—I thought you should know—they're taking the castle and Lady Mary is ill—very ill—and—and—"

He got to his feet. "Where is Lord Dunsten?"

"Lord Dunsten?"

He pushed her aside. "Get out of my way, stupid woman!"

He strode to the door and shouted. "Dunsten, come here!"

As if he had risen from the floor, Wells was suddenly there. And an instant later Lady Mary had slipped from her bed and Kate saw her standing in the door as Wells entered from the door opposite. She stared from one to the other, these three people, the ones she knew so well and scarcely recognized now.

"Here, Sir Richard," Wells called.

"Richard!" Lady Mary cried at the door. "You promised me you wouldn't go there again and you have—I can see you have! Ah, that's where you were in the night!"

Sir Richard looked at them blankly.

He put his hands to his forehead muttering, "I've had a strange dream—very strange!"

"You have been there again," Lady Mary insisted. She came in and clung to his arm. "What are you hiding in that place? Tell me—you must tell me. I heard something—someone talking—saying such strange things."

"You know what's there," he said. He tried to shake her off but she would not yield. "You've been there."

"I haven't been there for years."

"Books," he said. "Nothing but old books—and—and —a man's privacy."

"You're hiding something!"

"I have nothing," he cried with sudden anger. "Not even—a—a—a child. I don't have a child, I tell you!"

Her hands dropped from his arm. She said slowly, "You never forgive me, do you, Richard?"

"No one to—to—take my place . . . the throne," he muttered dully.

Wells stepped forward, shaking as if in a palsy, "Sir Richard, please, you're not yourself."

He led Sir Richard to a chair and helped him to be seated. "Lady Mary, if I may suggest—Kate, telephone Dr. Briggs, and fetch Mr. Webster. There's more here than you and I can manage— Don't stand there like stone!"

She felt like stone. The quarrel between these two whom she had never heard quarrel—what was this quarrel? *What throne?*

"Kate!" Wells shouted.

She looked into his angry eyes and, terrified, ran out of the room to the telephone and dialed frantically.

"Dr. Briggs? If you please—this is Kate at the castle. We're in great trouble, sir. . . . Both of them—like they were dreaming something. . . . No, sir, I never did see them like this. . . . Thank you, sir."

She put up the receiver and knocked on Philip Webster's door. He opened it immediately and came out dressed in his wrinkled tweeds but smelling of Pear's Soap.

"Ah, good morning, Kate."

"Please, Mr. Webster," she said breathlessly, "the Americans are acting as if they're taking the castle tomorrow."

"What!" he exclaimed.

"Yes, sir, and Sir Richard and Lady Mary are being very odd, too."

"Where are they?"

"In Sir Richard's room."

He strode off and she followed. When they reached the room, Kate could not believe what she saw. Wells was gone, and Sir Richard and Lady Mary were sitting at the small table by the window drinking tea together out of the same cup, as though there had been no quarrel. Webster paused at the door, unseen, and Kate waited behind him. The two at the table were talking together amicably.

"I tell you, my dear," Sir Richard was saying, "everything is quite all right. Blayne has my permission to take the measurements and so on. After all, he's not tearing down the castle. Nothing is settled yet and it's common sense that his men can't idle about. He's paying them, you know, and they may as well be doing something, even if it's no use in case we do not proceed. But if it troubles you, I'll have it all stopped, of course."

Lady Mary handed him the cup. "Do you want to get rid of the castle, Richard?"

Sir Richard waved the cup away. "You finish it, my dear." He felt for his pipe in his pocket. "It's you I think of—you couldn't live without the castle, could you now, my dear? Really, I mean."

Lady Mary considered. "One never knows," she said thoughtfully. "One never knows what one can do until one knows one must. In case one doesn't find the treasure—"

"You're not giving up, I hope," Sir Richard said. He lit his pipe and drew on it with enormous puffs of smoke. "It doesn't do to give up, you know. Certainly I never knew you to give up."

"I don't see anything wrong here," Webster said in a low voice and over his shoulder to Kate.

Nevertheless he entered the room. "Are you all right, Sir Richard?" he inquired.

Sir Richard looked up, surprised. "I? Oh quite! What makes you ask? Wonderful morning and all that! We've been having a little chat. Come in, Kate. I haven't seen you this morning. You're looking peaked— Isn't she, my dear?"

Kate had followed Webster into the room and stood there, puzzled, half awkward. Sir Richard reached for her hand.

"You should see the doctor, Kate. Her hand's hot, Webster." He fondled it a moment. They were all looking at her and she snatched her hand away. Sir Richard had never before taken her hand.

"Lady Mary," she said with determination. "You did say that last night you heard a real voice."

Lady Mary laughed. There was a tinge of pink in her cheeks. "Did I?"

Webster sat down quickly. "Ah yes—you were to find some sort of treasure, weren't you?"

Kate would not yield. "My lady, you said—"

"Did you or did you not find any treasure, my love?" Sir Richard inquired. "It's quite possible, you know, Webster. One does find the oddest things—the ruby, you remember—did I tell you I had it set in a heavy gold ring? I must show it to you. Kate, where did I put the ring?"

"I've never seen it," Kate said bluntly. "I never knew you had such a ring, Sir Richard."

"Oh come now," Sir Richard said. "Everybody's seen the ring. I'm immensely proud of it. I don't wear it all the time—it's much too conspicuous, unless one's a king, of course. . . . There's always that chance—"

"What chance?" Kate asked.

Sir Richard smiled. "The chance of—anything," he said, "the chance of finding a treasure, for example—or of selling the castle—or not selling it—" He flung out his hand in an expansive gesture.

Webster rose. "The next thing you know we'll be drawing up papers and asking for signatures."

"Perhaps it's the only way to break the hold of the past," Sir Richard said.

"But the treasure—"

"Yes, my love." He turned to Lady Mary indulgently. "It is said that every castle has a treasure."

"My lady! Sir Richard!" Kate gasped, but no one seemed to hear her.

"Such a nice young man," Lady Mary said softly. "I rather think I'd like to call him John. Would it be all right for me to do so, Richard?"

"It would indeed, my dear. After all, you have had some difficulty in remembering his proper name."

She smiled at him. "Not really, Richard. It's such a nice name, Blade. It makes me think of that sword lying on the tomb in the church. But John is nicer, so simple, and much easier to say."

"What are you waiting for, Kate?" Sir Richard asked suddenly and sharply.

Then they were all looking at Kate, smiling, kindly but remote and even cold. They had dismissed her, she knew, and she felt a wall rise between herself and them.

"Maybe I am mistaken in all of you," she said slowly. "Perhaps I don't know any of you. . . . I . . . I've only made a fool of myself . . . trying to do too much . . . thinking I was helping. I've insulted the American—and he's the only one who's been kind, after all." She heard someone give a sob and realized it was herself and she ran out of the room.

Halfway to her own room in the east wing, tears blinding her as she went, she felt herself suddenly caught in two strong arms.

"Whither so fast?" John Blayne demanded gaily.

"Oh—" She stopped and pulled away. "Please! I was going to find you as soon as I—I must tell you—I was quite wrong this morning." She was mopping at her eyes with the ruffled edge of her apron. "I overstepped myself. I had no right—being only the maid, to . . . to . . . to give orders as though I were . . ."

"Come here." He led her into an alcove where there was a stone seat under a high arched window. "Sit down."

He drew her down and handed her his large clean handkerchief. "Isn't this what the hero is always supposed to do? Provide a nice clean linen handkerchief to wipe the heroine's tears away? On second thought, I believe he's supposed to do the wiping. Kindly allow me— Ah, Kate, you take yourself so seriously, my child!"

What eyelashes she had, long and curling and black—no nonsense here about false ones and mascara and all that! He folded the handkerchief and put it in his pocket again.

"Now that's better, isn't it?"

She shook her head and bit her lip.

He looked grave. "Kate, listen to me. You keep reminding me that you are only the maid. You don't want me to forget it. You won't let me. Why?"

"Because"—she was very nearly crying again—"that's what I—am!"

He reached for her hand and held it on his open palm and looked at it, a small hand, plump like a child's hand, but strong. "It doesn't matter how many times you tell me," he said slowly. "It doesn't mean a thing to me, Kate. I'm an American. We don't classify people. You can live anywhere, be anybody, if you want to—if you are not too stubborn. That's a stubborn little thumb—it bends back too far."

He flexed her thumb. "I'm stubborn, too. See my thumb? I'm more stubborn than you—been at it longer so you may as well give up. You can't change me. And

I'm not going to take the castle away from you if you don't want me to have it. I'll go away and everything will be as it was before, as it always has been, always will be —and you'll be happy again."

"No," she said in a low voice. "I won't be happy again."

He folded his hand over her hand. "Your hand's trembling, trembling like a frightened bird. . . . Kate, tell me who you are. There's some secret here in the castle—I feel it. It's not about ghosts, either. It's about someone who's alive. . . . Let me help you."

"No secret." She shook her head.

"You don't want to tell me?"

"Only that I've been wrong—about you."

"But you don't know me."

"I've been mistaken about you. I mean—I thought you were—"

"What?"

He was gazing deep into her eyes and she could not look away. She tried to smile and felt herself blush and her heart beat. His face was near, very near—his lips—

"Kate!"

It was Wells. He stood there before them, his jaw hanging, his eyes stern. She snatched her hand away.

"Get back to the pantry at once," Wells ordered her. "The breakfast things are waiting, not to mention that this afternoon the public will be here."

John Blayne rose. "It's my fault, Wells. But I don't think you need speak to her like that, in any case."

Wells was icy. "And there's an overseas call for you, Mr. Blayne—it's waiting in the library—from your father again."

"Thanks." He paused to smile at Kate and sauntered toward the library.

Wells waited until he was out of sight, then turned to Kate. She was still sitting there in the deep window and now was looking out into the yew walk. "Don't get yourself mixed up with this American," he muttered. "There's enough wrong here in the castle without you confusing everything, too. Sir Richard would be very angry."

She did not turn her head. "It's a confusing world. I know—I agree with you, Grandfather. And I don't want to get—mixed up, as you call it. We're working people—that's all we are. They don't really care for us. Whatever they do, it's all above our heads. We'll never understand them."

"And you," he retorted heavily, "you don't know what you are talking about."

He left her and she watched his gaunt old figure shuffling down the long passage until it was out of sight. He had never loved her. Who was he? Who was she? Why were they so different, and why, for that matter, did she not love him? She had never loved him even as a child. She was always quite alone . . . but never so alone as now . . . and felt herself impelled, in loneliness, to follow John Blayne to find him blindly, merely to be near him for the brief time that he would still be here in the castle.

. . . He was in the library, sitting behind the great oak desk, his eyes shut, his face grimacing as he held the receiver as far as possible from him, as usual. From the receiver came his father's voice, loud and rasping.

"Do you hear me? . . . I want you back here in New York, next Monday. Why? For the merger, Johnny. Where have you been all this time?"

He replied reasonably but firmly. "It's not so simple, Dad. There are complications here—I don't understand them altogether, but—"

The voice cut across like a buzzsaw. "You won't be here, then?"

"I won't be there."

"Do you know what you're saying?" The voice took over again. "Louise's father will be mad, and when he gets mad you know what he's like! It makes me mad when he gets mad and between the two of us the merger will fall through again, like as not, the way it always does. What can I tell him now?"

"You don't need to give him any explanations for what I'm doing. What's all the opera about anyway?"

Kate tiptoed into the room. He did not see her and she stood waiting and silent.

"The opera," the voice emphasized each word, "is that Louise is running around with another man while you're running around a castle. If you're not here on Monday, you'll lose her, sure as my name is John Preston Blayne, Senior. Son, why do you throw everything away on a pile of rock?" The voice softened slightly. "You don't know what love is until you've lost it, the way I have. I remember everything I ever said to your mother that hurt her feelings. It's not just what I said or did, either. It's the times I could have been with her and wasn't, the things I wish now I'd done . . ."

The grating voice faltered and recovered. "To hell with you," it said distinctly, and there was the bang of the receiver.

Kate tried to escape unseen, but he strode between her and the door. "That was my father."

"I know."

"You're not going before I explain?"

"About mergers?"

"No, something much more important."

She looked at him bravely. Then she went to the desk, took up the receiver and held it out to him. "Here," she said, "take it."

He took it stupidly. "What for?"

"Isn't there a cable you should send first?"

She walked out of the room, her head held high, and

left him staring after her. He took a few steps in her direction, then stopped and walked slowly back to the desk. He sat down and held his head in his hands. Ten minutes passed. He reached again for the receiver, dialed, and waited. Then he sent his message, not to his father but to Louise.

He sat a moment longer, then smiled suddenly and slapped the desk with both hands. To the tune of a waltz whistled under his breath, he all but danced out of the room.

. . . In her own room Kate sat down and wept. She was out of breath and tired and bewildered. It was a tower room, the western tower, a circle of narrow windows and a small fireplace set low in the gray rock walls. It had once belonged to a maid-of-honor, a very young one, whose home had been in Wales and who, because she was lonely, had hanged herself one night from the broad beam in the center of the ceiling. No one had missed her and it had been days before they thought to look for her. Megan was her name, and Kate had thought of her often, had wondered how she looked and whether there was another reason than loneliness to make her want to die. Perhaps her mistress had been cruel, perhaps she had been in love, perhaps—perhaps—but who knew?

It seemed to her now that she understood how it was that Megan had died in this little room. Perhaps she too had sat weeping on this very stool of oak set by the chimney piece. She was not herself quite ready to die but she wanted to weep and did weep now with long, satisfying sobs until she could no more. Then she got up and washed her face and tidied her hair and after that she opened her chest of drawers and made everything in them neat. This done she sewed on two buttons that had fallen from her wool jacket and mended a rent in her black silk slip. She could think of nothing more to do then, and she opened the door and listened to know how they were managing in the castle without her. Silence was all she heard, and after listening for a moment she tiptoed down the circular stairs and slipped across to the great hall where there was plenty of noise and bustle, John's voice asking questions, demanding, arguing, contradicting; other voices replying.

"We must provide an incentive," he was saying. "What, for example, could we do here after the castle is gone? How could the land be used most profitably?"

"You're providing incentive in the cash sum you're offering, aren't you?"

The voice belonged to David Holt, the tall gray-haired man in a neat business suit. He sat at a long table beside John and they were studying figures from a big black book.

"I want a project," John went on. "Cash is no good these days. Something to keep people at work and earning would be the thing."

One of the young men stopped by. "Know what, Mr. Blayne? Under three feet of topsoil this whole hill is clay! Cement works is the answer. Rebuild all these old huts. Look at the way they did Park Avenue at home! Steel and glass and cement! Handsome."

John laughed. "Another New York? Isn't one enough?"

"You could make a park, Mr. Blayne," another young man sang from the opposite side of the hall. "Disneyland, England! They need something to make 'em laugh, in my opinion. Public recreation."

"Jot down the ideas, Holt," John said to the lawyer. "I've been thinking myself of a model farm. That wouldn't spoil the landscape. Milk parlors, silos, everything. It's developed country you know, but jungles and castles can be equally unproductive."

"Are you serious?"

"But certainly! I don't want to leave a desert behind

me. Let's really go into it for the heck of it. Have the fellows make some drawings just in case—estimate the costs—the most up-to-date machinery, and Guernsey herds brought from U.S.A. There's something romantic about that! Guernseys came from the Isle of Guernsey but like the rest of us they've been improved by their sojourn in America. So we return them in their modern shape. Meantime I'm not discarding any ideas. We have a week to—"

Kate on her way back to the kitchen caught the word. A week! Was he staying a week longer? She put her hands to her lips in an involuntary gesture. How could she bear it? Let him go now while she still had her heart in control! She went quickly down the passage to Lady Mary and Sir Richard in their private sitting room. It must be almost time for luncheon and she had been away wickedly long. They'd been calling her, doubtless. But no, they were sitting placidly by the window, he smoking his pipe and she at her crocheting again, as mild as though there had been no morning commotion. Philip Webster was pacing the floor, his hands in his pockets and his gray hair a tangle, as if he had thrust his hands through it too often.

Lady Mary signed to Kate that she was not needed, and Kate turned and went to her duties in pantry and kitchen.

"You could sell parts of the estate, you know, Richard."

"I'll not sell," Sir Richard said. "I'll fight to the end. . . . My dear"—he turned to Lady Mary—"you shall keep your realm whole. It is your realm, you know, this little kingdom—after all, there are such small realms— Monaco, Liechtenstein and now Starborough—it's not unreasonable. You can depend upon me. I shan't let the tenants get the upper hand. I've been too soft with them. What was it John Gomer said? 'Three things, all of the same sort, are merciless when they get the upper hand: a waterflood, a wasting fire, and the common multitude of small folk.' The year was 1385, but what he said is as true today."

"I don't know what you're talking about, Richard," Lady Mary said absently. She was counting stitches. "Oh bother, I've done it wrong." She began to unravel.

"If I should sell off bits and patches," Sir Richard said, "people would move in. They'd build houses. The castle would be standing alone in the midst of a village."

"I suppose they would," Lady Mary observed, crocheting again.

"We'd be besieged," Sir Richard went on, "but it wouldn't be the first time, you know, Webster, and the castle can be defended. The moat is dry, of course, but that's because it was drained against the mosquitoes. It would be easy to debouch the brook again as it was and the moat would fill up quickly. Essential, too, for people would swarm over the battlements otherwise! I planned it all, long ago."

Webster sat down suddenly and stared at him. "You're talking rot, Richard."

"Indeed I am not," Sir Richard retorted. His ruddy face was alight and his eyes glittered under his heavy brows. "It certainly is not rot for an Englishman to defend his castle. It's his duty, he's the king. It wouldn't be the first time a king has stood on the tower balcony of Starborough Castle and commanded his men until they forced a retreat!"

Lady Mary looked up from the pink wool. "Who would retreat, Richard?" Her voice was quiet and suddenly her face was sad.

He stared at her blankly. "People, you know—their houses—"

"What houses?"

"The houses people would build."

"Houses won't walk away," she said in the same sad
and quiet voice. "And they aren't the enemy."

"They are," he cried. "They stifle me! They stifle great-
ness! That's why kings always build their castles far away
in lonely places. The Commons! That's the enemy. The
common people—the fools—the serfs—the—the—I tell
you, I'll defend this castle as long as I live! I'll never
leave it—"

She interrupted. "Do you know what they'll do then?
They'll pull down the castle. It can't stand here alone.
In the end they'll tear it down—or make it into something
useful for themselves. It's been here too long. I am beginning to know that."

"Perhaps you are right, Lady Mary," Webster said.

Sir Richard was on his feet again. His brain was suddenly a burning torture inside his skull. "You two," he
muttered, "you two—against me! Where's Wells?"

He stamped out of the room.

In the silence Lady Mary continued to crochet and
Webster was silent.

"It was he," Lady Mary said at last, "it was Richard
who brought the Americans here, Philip—wasn't it?"

"Certainly it was he who wanted me to advertise,"
Webster said.

"Now he doesn't want to leave. A moment ago he said
he was doing it for me. I don't really care anymore. . . .
It's only for him. . . . But there's something else, it
seems. . . . Perhaps we're coming to the bottom of things
at last."

Webster breathed hard, as though he were choking. "I
don't understand, Lady Mary."

"I don't understand either, Philip, not even Richard, it
seems, with whom I have lived all these years. We've been
happy, or I thought we had. I'm not sure about that,
either, now. And I've always believed—foolishly, I daresay—that somehow . . . somebody . . . would help us.

Perhaps *they* can't. Perhaps it's too hard for *them*, too. I don't think *they've* really gone anywhere, you know, in spite of being dead. Philip, *they're* just in another state of consciousness. But that's the same as being in another country, I suppose—it really is. I'm very sorry for *them*, consequently. But we can't depend on *them*. We must look after ourselves."

Webster stared at her with round and wondering eyes. "I don't know what you're talking about now, Lady Mary."

"No, I suppose you don't." Lady Mary sighed and put her work away into a small wicker basket.

The door opened and Wells entered. He had brushed his hair and put on a white shirt under his worn uniform, but he looked drawn and ill and very old.

"If you please, my lady," he said, "what about the American? Do we have him for meals all day?"

His voice quivered and Lady Mary looked at him. "What's wrong with you, Wells? You look as though you'd—you'd seen something."

Wells put his hand to his mouth to hide his trembling lips. "I heard Sir Richard talking to you, my lady. He's upset with me, really—not with you—I know it. But indeed I can't do everything he wants done. He needs better supporters than I can be at my age, my lady. I'm no longer a proper protector for him. . . ." Suddenly he began to mumble. "The King needs help. I can't do it alone —I can't—I can't . . ."

"What king?" Lady Mary demanded.

Wells fumbled for his handkerchief and wiped his eyes before he answered. "I beg your pardon, my lady?"

"I asked what king," Lady Mary repeated distinctly.

"I don't know what you mean, my lady. I was talking of Sir Richard."

Webster turned to Wells. "You mean you can't run this place any longer alone, don't you?"

"Yes, sir," Wells said. "Thank you, sir. But if I could just speak with you, my lady—alone, for a minute."

Lady Mary sat with her hands folded in her lap and her head sunk on her breast. She looked up now and spoke with sharp irritation. "No, no, Wells. I don't want to talk now. Of course we must have the American. We shall all sit down to luncheon together."

"There are six Americans, my lady."

"And three of us. That will be nine, Wells."

She dismissed him with a nod and with another nod to Webster she rose and walked down the passage to Sir Richard's room. He was not there but if he had been, she thought, she would have entered just the same. The time had come for her to discover for herself what had happened in his mind and memory. She walked across the empty room to the paneled wall and tried to open it. It could move, that she knew, although this only by hearsay. She pressed each panel, each point in the carving, each possible indentation, but it remained as it was.

"Come now," she murmured. "You do open, you know —don't pretend with me, please! I've lived here too long."

Still it resisted and she was about to give up when suddenly at her touch, she did not know where, the wall slid back noiselessly—and she was face to face with Sir Richard. He stood there looking at her as though she were a stranger, an interloper. His face was proud and cold and he held himself tensely erect, his hands at his sides. She stared at him. The blood drained away from her head and heart and she felt faint. She tried to cry out and could not. With a great effort she summoned her strength.

"I am glad I have found you at last, Richard. I've been looking for you such a long time—all my life, I think!"

She spoke the words as though she had expected to find him there and she waited for him to reply. Instead he put out his hand and touched the panel. It slid between them without noise, swiftly and smoothly, and she was left standing alone.

For a moment she was shocked, then galvanized by anger. This was not to be endured! How dared he shut her out as though she were a stranger? What was wrong with him? She felt a horrible panic of fear. She pounded on the panel with her fists and screamed.

"Richard, let me in! Richard—Richard—"

There was no answer. She laid her ear to the panel. No sound—nothing! In the ivy outside the open window the birds fluttered their wings and flew away.

"I must find him," she muttered, frantic, and tried again to find the knob in the carving, the secret spot, which would open the wall, but however she pressed and pushed and felt the paneled surface she could not find it. There was no other way in which to get behind the panel—or was there? She tried to remember, her eyes closed, her hands pressed to her temples. Long ago, when she came to the castle a bride, Richard had taken her one day to a tower room, the throne room, he had called it, because when he was a little boy he had played at being king with his father, his crippled father. But there had been no throne in that room—only a heavy old chair.

How had they got there that day, she and Richard? And why had she never gone there again? Ah, but she hadn't wanted to! She had not forgotten, though she had never allowed herself to think of it, the change that had come over him, Richard suddenly brooding, resentful, sad. She saw his beautiful young face even now and heard his voice across the years.

"I'm glad you never saw my father. He was hideously wounded in the war. Lucky I was born before he left or I'd never been born at all!"

She had been too young, then, too much a child, to

understand or to reply. She had stood staring at him and he had rushed on.

"He was proud of me—sickeningly proud of my—my looks—and everything. He kept wanting me to marry young—to have sons. I wouldn't marry just to provide heirs, I told him—not until I met you. And now it's too late—he's dead and he'll never see our children."

She remembered how frightened she had been when he gave a great sob. She had never seen a man weep and she had put her arms about him and comforted him. "Richard, darling, we'll have lots of beautiful children— I promise!"

She wept now, silently, forcing back her own sobs. She had not been able to keep the promise—there had been no children. It was intolerable, this pain of remembrance. She hastened blindly from the room, down the passage in what direction she did not think. She saw Kate in a doorway with a tray of dishes in her hands; at the sight of her startled face Lady Mary broke into a run. It was years since she had really run as fast as she could. Her heart beat against her ribs but she ran on and on by instinct, like a homing pigeon, down the stairs that led to the dungeon—and found herself stopped by the same great door, closed and blocking her way. It was the door behind which she had heard voices. She listened now, both hands clenched on her breast, and heard nothing. She beat on the door and shouted as loudly as she could.

"Richard—Richard!"

There was no answer. Why did she call Richard? The voices had nothing to do with him—or did they? Ah, the door was immovably closed! Her strength gave out and she leaned her arms against it and her head on her arms and felt that she would die of faintness. And then she felt strong arms about her and heard Kate's voice.

"My lady—my lady, whatever! Lucky the doctor's come at this very moment. It's Dr. Broomhall, my lady, the young doctor—old Dr. Briggs said he had to go to London for the day when I called. I followed you as soon as I could set my tray down. You looked ghastly when you ran past me, not seeing anything. When the doctor stepped in the door and I told him—"

The doctor, close behind Kate, interrupted. "Really, Lady Mary, this is very shocking. I'm told you're in bed and here I find you in this damp hole, running about—"

"Richard," she gasped. "Find Sir Richard—look after him—"

"Yes my lady," Kate said soothingly, "yes, indeed we will, but all the same you shouldn't have—"

"She's to go to her room at once," the doctor ordered.

He seized one arm and Kate the other, and they marched Lady Mary between them, half carrying her.

"You're so uneven," Lady Mary murmured, dazed.

"Eh?" Dr. Broomhall was a young man, red-haired and lean and strong.

"You're too tall," Lady Mary said fretfully, "much too tall and Kate's short—like—crutches that—don't match."

He laughed a loud healthy shout. "Six foot four—I agree that's too tall, Allow me, Lady Mary." And with one sweep of his arm he caught her up and carried her as lightly as though she were a child. She felt suddenly better.

"Oh, mercy," she murmured. "I haven't been carried like this since my honeymoon. Richard used to tease me by taking me off my feet. I'm not sure I should allow you—"

"There's not much wrong with her," the doctor said to Kate over his shoulder.

"It's Richard who wants looking after," Lady Mary said.

"What's wrong with him?" the doctor asked, half joking. "He looked very fit when I saw him in the village yesterday, trotting along the street on that fine gray horse of his!"

"I'm frightened."

She closed her eyes and repeated in a whisper. "Very frightened. He's—odd."

"Odd?" The doctor's voice was quiet and the mirth gone.

"He . . . he looked at me as though he hadn't seen me before. . . . And he shut a . . . a door in my face. When I called he . . . he . . . didn't answer."

"Was he down in the dungeon, too?"

"No. I ran down . . . when he wouldn't open the . . . the door . . . there's an old stone staircase that leads into the . . . the . . . the . . ."

"The what?"

"I don't know. A sort of room—"

Lady Mary fell silent. Dr. Broomhall's eyes met Kate's in a significant glance. Something is wrong here, the glance said. She nodded. They had arrived at the door of Lady Mary's room. Kate opened it and he carried her in and laid her upon the bed. But she sat up suddenly and cried out.

"Richard!"

For there Sir Richard stood in the middle of the room, as though he were waiting for her entrance.

"My dear," he said, coming forward. "Where have you been? I've looked everywhere for you. One of the men said he saw you coming in this direction and so I came here, only to find you gone."

"Richard," she whispered, staring at him as though he were a ghost. "Why did you lock the panel?"

He lifted his brushy red-gray eyebrows. "Panel? What panel?"

"Richard, don't pretend!"

"I'm not pretending, my dear. It's you—you don't feel well, obviously—Doctor, she's not well."

Before the doctor could agree, there was a knock at the half-open door and John Blayne entered.

"Ah, you found her," he said. "The men told me you were lost, Lady Mary. They've all been looking for you. Where was she, Kate?"

"In the dungeon," Kate said gravely.

"Good God!" Sir Richard exclaimed. "When will you give up that absurd treasure hunt? You might have fallen —the stone floors are slippery with damp—you've got a chill. Lie down, dear."

He pushed Lady Mary gently back on the pillows and chafed her hands and reproached Kate the while.

"Kate, how could you let her out of your sight?"

"She said you had shut her out somewhere," Kate said bluntly.

"I shut her out? How absurd—I was here all the time," Sir Richard said. "Why did she run to the dungeon?"

"We had been down there before," Kate faltered. "To . . . to look for the treasure."

"You weren't serious!" John exclaimed. "I thought it was all in joke."

"We were serious!" Kate said. She looked from one face to the other and flushed.

"At Lady Mary's age—" the doctor began but Sir Richard cut him off.

"It's not a matter of age. She's always had strange notions about—well, yes, perhaps it's been worse lately. . . . Kate, let there be no more nonsense about a treasure. I won't have her worried. It's my responsibility— How is she, Doctor?"

The doctor had been examining Lady Mary, her eyes, her pulse, and now he took a powder from his case which stood on the floor where he had left it.

"She's had a mild shock of some kind," he said, "and she wants rest. Take this now, Lady Mary. It's only a mild sedation. You'll sleep for a bit and wake, feeling better. I suggest that we all leave the room. She's having too much excitement."

"I shan't leave her," Sir Richard said with decision.

"Very well, then the rest of us," the doctor said. "I'll call again later in the day."

He led the way, John and Kate following, and they walked softly out of the room. Sir Richard drew a chair to the bedside and sat down. He stroked her hand gently and Lady Mary looked at him with pleading, doubting eyes.

"Was I dreaming, Richard?" she said faintly. "Didn't you . . . weren't you . . . behind the panel when I—"

He interrupted her. "My dear, you are simply to stop worrying. I shall attend to everything. In due course, I'll take care of everything. Close your eyes, you're safe in your own room, in our own home, our castle—"

"I don't think it was a dream."

"One has all sorts of dreams—there's nothing wrong with dreams," Sir Richard said.

His voice was far away and she could only just hear what he said. But perhaps it did not matter, perhaps it was true that she had only dreamed. He would take care of her. . . . And she drifted away into a realm of peace.

And Sir Richard sat there beside her, stroking her hand rhythmically, lovingly, and murmuring to her with tenderness as he gazed at her sleeping face.

"You're so pale, poor darling . . . I must take care of you. And I can, I've kept it a secret from you—I still can't tell you."

He leaned toward her, his face close to hers. "Do you hear me, my love?"

Her eyelids would not open. They were too heavy to lift. She could not speak. This unutterable weariness, lying like a weight of lead on her body—she could only hear his voice echoing in her ears.

"She doesn't hear," he was muttering. "Just as well . . .

the crown is my responsibility . . . my fault . . . I'm a weakling. I should have dealt with my enemies the way Father did, with a sword! . . . I've waited too long. I was afraid to be called a monster as he was, poor crippled king! But I'll be worthy of my name at last—Richard the Fourth!"

He dropped her hand and left her side and began to pace about the room aimlessly, stooping to stare at the bowl of spring flowers on a small desk of rosewood, at the silver brushes on the dressing table, at his own photograph, himself as a young man, framed in gold and hung on the eastern wall.

"Handsome, I suppose—I was called that—even my father—But he said I was weak. I wasn't, I'm not—he was a monster—no, not a monster. He knew how to deal with people. I don't—I don't want to—but you must be strong—you must—"

He leaned toward the photograph and stared into his own gay young face.

"You're weak—weak—hiding yourself, not telling even your queen! She's lying there on the bed—ill, unconscious—your daughter defiled—even your son killed by foreigners, your only son—alone in London—an outpost —why wasn't he here in the castle—safe? You didn't dare—you and your secrets—you let the prince be killed —the foreigner is here—here in the castle where you've been hiding all these years. I hate you!"

He smashed the picture with his fist. The glass broke and crashed to the floor. He stood staring at the ruins.

"My father's sword," he muttered.

From far away Lady Mary heard the crash. She struggled upward against the enveloping darkness of sleep. She opened her eyes and saw him turn blindly toward the door, his face flushed, his eyes unseeing. She forced herself to cry out.

"Richard, Richard—you're—"

Ill was what she wanted to say—*Richard, you're ill. Come, let me care for you. Someone come and help us both.* She thought she had screamed but her voice had not left her throat. She tried to get up, to run after him, and could not move. She was pulled back into sleep and unconsciousness.

. . . Before Dr. Broomhall left the castle he spoke privately with Kate. "I am not so concerned about Lady Mary," he said, "her indisposition is temporary, the result of a fright and exposure, and a certain amount of exhaustion. She will be quite herself when she comes out of her sleep in a few hours. Keep her warm and as quiet as possible and"—he smiled encouragingly—"free from worry."

"I'll do my best, Dr. Broomhall. And Sir Richard?"

"He is the one about whom I am really concerned, though I must wait for Dr. Briggs to return from London to discuss the case."

"But he seemed . . ."

Dr. Broomhall shook his head. "Whatever he said in his own self-defense was negated by the expression in his eyes. Quite obviously he is subject to delusions. How long has this been going on, Kate?"

"I . . . I can't rightly say, sir."

"With Lady Mary, a sudden shock caused her trouble; but with Sir Richard the delusions are functional and thus their treatment is not so simple."

"What would you mean by that, sir?"

"Emotionally determined and reaching over a considerable period of time." He glanced around him. "It's beautiful, this old castle, but I wish Sir Richard and Lady Mary could get away from it for a while, a good long while. When the past begins to affect the present, as it would seem to be doing with Sir Richard, its hold should be broken. But, as I said, I will have to discuss this with Dr. Briggs."

"Thank you, sir."

"Do the best you can for them, Kate, and I'll come by again within a few hours to see how Lady Mary is." He turned and went toward his small car that had been standing behind the Americans' large one.

Half an hour later, luncheon was announced. Sir Richard was nowhere to be found, and as his horse was not in the stable it could only be assumed that he had gone for a canter. Lady Mary was deep in sleep. Philip Webster sat down at the long table with the six Americans and luncheon was served by Wells and Kate. They did not linger over their coffee. Wells had reminded them all that this was the day the castle was open to the public and by three o'clock the charabancs would arrive.

"There'll be people all over the place," Wells said dismally, "as you well know, Mr. Webster."

"That I do, Wells, and I'll not be one of them. I'm going to the inn to do some telephoning. How about you, Mr. Holt, may I offer you a ride in my Austin?"

"You may indeed, Mr. Webster. I, too, have business to transact that can best be done in the relative quiet of the village inn. John?"

"I'll stay here with the boys. We'll work until we hear the buses, then we'll make ourselves scarce. Sir Richard got out ahead of us all, didn't he?"

"He often does this, sir," Wells said apologetically. "He can't abide having these people in his castle. Invaders, he calls them, though they're most of them British and they pay good money."

. . . Sir Richard, without benefit of Wells, changed into his riding clothes; then he strode rapidly through the familiar passages of the castle, out the wide west door, and across the lawn to the stable. Again, without benefit of

Wells, he led his gray stallion from the stall, saddled and bridled him, and mounted with the ease of one long accustomed to horses. He ran his hand down the smooth neck and spoke in a low tone. The stallion pricked his ears and flicked his tail. His iron-shod hooves echoed on the cobbles of the stable yard, then thudded softly on the grass as he yielded to the direction given him. Trotting first, then breaking into an easy gallop, he carried his master over greening meadows and along lanes still starry with primroses.

Half an hour later, Sir Richard reined up by the church and dismounted. Before looping the reins over the hitching post he put his hand to his head to quiet the pain that had begun its raging. Usually a brisk ride made the pain abate, sometimes even cease, but this was not the case today.

The church was dim and empty, as he knew it would be in the early afternoon. He walked up the center aisle and turned to the alcove at the left of the altar. There his ancestors were buried; there he would lie someday with Mary beside him, the last of the Sedgeleys. At one side was the tomb of his father. Upon it lay a bronze statue in a coat of mail, gauntleted hands folded across the breast. Placed close to the figure and filling the space from shoulder to knee was the sword of his ancestor William Sedgeley, the man to whom the castle had been given five centuries ago. Tradition said it lay there ready to be used, but only by a Sedgeley and only in a moment of utter need.

Sir Richard stood by the tomb, then he put his right hand on the sword and drew it from its scabbard. It came with difficulty, but he put his strength to it and the sound it made as metal scraped against metal echoed in the silence of the church. He lifted it in his hands, bent his lips to the hilt, then held it upright before him.

"I swear," he began, in a loud hoarse voice, "I swear, by my father and by my forefathers—"

"Sir Richard!"

There, coming up the altar steps, was the vicar.

"Yes, it is I, Sir Richard Sedgeley of Starborough Castle."

"You surprised me, Sir Richard," the vicar said uncertainly, peering into the shadows of the alcove. "I thought I heard an unusual sound and came to investigate."

"You see Richard the Fourth," Sir Richard said stiffly, the sword still upright before him.

"I beg your pardon?" the vicar asked. He stared at the strange figure, at the flushed face and blazing eyes, the upright sword. "Are you quite yourself, Sir Richard?" he inquired, frightened.

"Richard the Third was my father, the crippled king, you remember! His armies were very strong. He could wield the sword easily. And I am here to claim the sword," Sir Richard declared in an unearthly voice.

So speaking, he pushed the vicar aside and left the church, the sword held high in his right hand.

". . . You'll not get up, my lady," Kate declared, "even though the tourists are coming this afternoon."

"But I am up," Lady Mary said crossly. "What's more, I'm half dressed. Go away, Kate."

"I will not," Kate retorted.

After serving luncheon and finishing her work in the pantry, Kate had come straight to Lady Mary's room expecting to find her still asleep, or perhaps drowsily waking. She had found Lady Mary sitting on the edge of her bed, trying to put on her clothes. Remonstrances were of no avail, her ladyship was adamant.

"Kate, I tell you, I must see that American. I have something to talk about—business—it's very important. Where is he?"

"The doctor gave me my orders," Kate said stubbornly. "You're to stay in bed, my lady. Tomorrow, if you feel——"

"Tomorrow will be too late," Lady Mary said, gently stubborn. "And how dare you talk about orders, Kate? You forget yourself, indeed you do. I'm surprised at you. You're getting above yourself, you really are. I've noticed it before. We've spoiled you, and now, just because we're in difficulties you're behaving very badly. You're taking advantage."

Kate stared at her astonished and burst into tears. Never before had Lady Mary spoken like this. "Oh, my lady, you know that I can't bear seeing you and Sir Richard in trouble."

"I must speak with that American. I want to tell him to go at once. It's he who has caused all this trouble."

"Oh, I agree that the American should leave us," Kate wailed. "I do want him to go, all of them to go. If we could only get back to the sweet old days, dear, with just the three of us here, and Wells, so peaceful it was." She continued to sob.

"Do stop crying, Kate," Lady Mary said impatiently. "It upsets me. You know we can't do without you, whatever you are. Now help me with my things, for my head does feel a bit heavy. Mind that button, it's almost off. Now, that's better—I'm properly dressed. Take me to the American, wherever he may be." She leaned on Kate's arm and talked as they walked together.

They found him on the terrace in consultation with one of his young men. Lady Mary straightened her frail body. She lifted her head and her eyes shone blue. "Mr. Blayne!"

"Yes, Lady Mary." He smiled good-naturedly. "If you've come to tell me to go I want to assure you that we will be off at precisely five minutes to three."

Lady Mary looked at the young men inside the castle

who were making measurements and drawing sketches on large pieces of paper. "Those Americans seem to be everywhere," she said, "don't you think so, Kate?"

"I haven't thought about it, my lady," Kate said.

"You should think, you know, Kate," she went on with gentle severity. "Everyone should think these days, if at all possible, about everything. Which reminds me, Mr. Blayne, would you mind leaving immediately instead of when the tourists come?"

He stood there bemused, wondering if he was being made game of in some obscure English fashion.

"Leave, Lady Mary?"

"Please do so," Lady Mary said in the same pleasant voice. "With all cohorts! Kate, tell the men that Mr. Blayne is leaving, at my request."

"They won't listen to me, my lady. I tried that before," Kate said.

There had been enough of this game, whatever it was, and John broke in impetuously. "Of course we will leave, Lady Mary, but I must remind you that Sir Richard gave us permission to remain—in fact, he asked us to proceed with the castle as planned, and—"

Lady Mary drew herself up so suddenly that she tottered. Kate stepped forward to offer her arm, and Lady Mary steadied herself. Indignation enlivened her whole being.

"How dare you," she cried. "Do you question who I am? This is my home, Mr. Blayne—I have the right to—to—"

"We go at once."

"Kate," Lady Mary said imperiously, "go with him, else he'll lose his way." She lowered her voice. "And he's not to go near Sir Richard, mind you. If you see Wells, send him here at once."

"Yes, my lady," Kate said, and followed John Blayne. Instead of going immediately to inform the rest of his young men, he had gone into the garden. She caught up with him near one of the elephant yews. For a moment they looked at each other without speaking.

"Kate, what does this mean?" He spoke impatiently. "And how am I to know what to do? Sir Richard tells me to stay, Lady Mary tells me to go, and both of them act as if they were living in the Middle Ages when people could be ordered around."

"In a way they are living back in the past, Mr. Blayne, that's what's the trouble. It's the castle—they've got to get away from it."

"There may be a way, though it may not be the eternal way," he reminded her. He reached out and took her hand, holding it in his palm like a flower. "Do you know you have pretty little hands?"

"Please—" She blushed and tried to pull her hand away, but he covered it with his other hand.

"Why do you distrust Americans?" he inquired.

"I don't," she said. "Not at all," she added. "Why should I? You are the only one I know."

Oh, what a pretty girl she is, he thought. Assured and graceful and proud-looking, her face was a picture with its straight features, fine skin and violet eyes.

"Then why don't you trust me?"

"Please, Mr. Blayne—"

He saw the look in her eyes and let her hand slip away. "Kate, what is it?"

She bit her lip and tears brimmed her eyes. "It's just that I . . ." She faltered, paused.

"Just that you what?" He tipped her head up to look at him, his forefinger under her chin, but she twisted away from him.

"There, it's nothing—it's more than just the castle. Sir Richard and Lady Mary grieve so only about the castle. I have to think of them, you know, take care of them—"

"It's the treasure in the castle, isn't it?" he asked.

She took him seriously. "Yes, yes, I expect it is."

"Have you any idea what that treasure is?"

For a moment she looked almost frightened as his eyes kept their steady gaze on her. "N-no, no I haven't, Mr.—"

"John," he interrupted.

"John," she repeated, like a child learning a new word in school.

"I'm just beginning to understand."

"I wish you would go away, really I do," she said in a low voice. "I wish you would leave us to ourselves."

"You mustn't blame me, you know, Kate. It's not my fault, and my going away won't solve anything. If you'd only explain—"

She interrupted him in sudden impatience. "I can't explain, I tell you. I'm only the maid."

"You're not! You're everything here in the castle and I can't leave you," he said firmly. "Here I stay, until—"

She could be firm, too. "You're not. You're going, as Lady Mary asked you to."

He yielded suddenly, seeing that neither was to be gainsaid. "We go at once," he said.

. . . Presently Wells stood before Lady Mary. "You sent for me, my lady?"

"I did. I want to know where Sir Richard is."

His eyelids flickered. "I do not know, my lady. He went off on his horse before luncheon. Will that be all?"

"You should know. It's your duty, Wells, always to know where Sir Richard is."

"I've a good deal to do, my lady."

"Don't speak to me like that!"

"No, my lady. I'm sorry, my lady."

She paused, to signify he was not forgiven, then went on, "Go and find him."

"Yes, my lady."

He had walked as far as the entrance to the castle when suddenly she called him back.

"Wells, come here!"

He came back slowly, his gnarled hands hanging at his sides, surprise on his long, old face.

"Wells," she said in a low hurried voice, "I understand —what I didn't before."

He looked blank.

"Wells!" she said sharply.

"Yes, my lady?"

"I know everything!"

"Everything, my lady?"

"Everything. . . . Wells, I saw him."

The look on the long face changed. The cheeks quivered, he blinked his eyes rapidly two or three times, he wet his lips before he spoke.

"Then I can only say I'm glad, my lady. It's been a strain—fearful, I might say."

"I'm sure it has been. You did what you thought was right. I don't blame you."

She paused. Her face quivered piteously and he looked away, in tender respect. She went on, hurrying her words, her voice low.

"Wells, the boy—Colin—wasn't yours, was he?"

"No, my lady—"

"Then, why did you—"

"For his mother, my lady. Elsie, that was. I was daft about her. In love, that is. . . . She wouldn't look at me, though she knew Sir Richard couldn't—his father would never have allowed a farmer's daughter to—"

"Stop for a moment, Wells."

She looked so desperately pale that he was frightened and yet he dared not call anyone. To think that all these years she had not known! He'd wondered, but Elsie had said no, she didn't know—not Lady Mary.

"Don't take it hard now, my lady," he whispered. "It was all done with long ago."

"Did he—love her, Wells?"

"Sir Richard? Oh no, my lady—it was just a fancy, on a summer's day. Even she knew that. And she—she was afraid of him, in a way, so far above her station."

"But she gave him a son."

Wells hesitated. "Well, in a manner of speaking. The child was a boy—yes, my lady."

"So it *was* my fault that—"

She was wiping her eyes on a wisp of lace handkerchief which she pulled from her belt.

"What was your fault, my lady?"

She shook her head and could not answer for a moment.

"You must help me, Wells," she said at last.

"Anything, my lady."

"We must get rid of the Americans, or have they gone already?"

"I couldn't say, my lady. I've been in the kitchen. I'm putting together a lamb stew for dinner—"

"Come with me now. We must find Sir Richard."

She put out her hand to lean on his arm as they went into the castle.

. . . The four young men were folding their papers into their briefcases, laughing, ironical.

"No explanations?"

"Command from the brass, that's all! Be out of here in fifteen minutes—said he'd meet us at the inn."

"Waste of time from the beginning—"

"Not if we're paid for it—"

"Look at the old lady coming in—and the old ghost—"

They stared at Lady Mary as she stood watching them.

"Make haste, if you please," she said coldly.

"Nothing suits us better, lady."

"Impudence," she muttered, but they heard her.

"Damn the Americans, eh, lady? Send us to hell, if it's America, that is—"

"Move on, Wells."

From room to room they went, but nowhere was there a glimpse of Sir Richard. Ahead of them Kate and John were walking side by side.

At the door John stopped. Her face, so sweetly young, so childlike when she was hurt, was upturned to him now, lips quivering, eyes misted—those violet eyes, he thought as he looked deep into them.

"Where will you go?" she asked.

"To the inn in the village."

"Shall we never meet again?"

"Is there any reason for us to meet, Kate?" He stood looking down at the upturned face. He had not fully realized until now that she was only a little thing. She was always so brisk, so vivid, so busy, that she had seemed taller than she was. Now, the briskness gone, the vivacity subdued, she looked small and helpless. He wanted to take her hand and did not.

"I suppose not," she said. "I can't think of any reason except—" She bit her lip.

"Except what, Kate?"

"In a queer sort of way," she said haltingly, "I shall—miss you. Silly, because of course you won't be missing me."

"In a queer sort of way," he said, gazing at her steadily, "I shall miss you."

He took her hand now in both of his. "Good-bye, little Kate," he said.

"Good-bye," she said, her voice a whisper.

He ran down the steps to his long green car. He got in and turned to wave before he drove off. Kate smiled as his lips shaped the words, "I'm not leaving for good."

Then Lady Mary, accompanied by Wells, joined Kate

on the steps. She held up her frail hand to wave. John Blayne gazed at the three of them with strange premonition, with strange regret. What would become of them? What would become of Kate? The sun was high above the western tower and the golden light flamed over the dark stone walls. Their figures all looked small and helpless in the shadow of the castle.

The soft purr of the engine beat like a heart alive and Kate, hearing it and knowing who was behind that wheel, was filled with a forlorn sadness. Never had she felt so alone. Instinctively her hands flew to her cheeks in a gesture of fright. How could she stay here now? How could she bear never to see him again? Watching her, John Blayne was impelled by the same instinct to cut off the engine, open the door of the car and dash back to her.

Yet when he reached them it was to Lady Mary he spoke. "Lady Mary, please, I beg you, can I be of help to Sir Richard? Is something seriously the matter?"

She was surprised, agitated. "No, no, please go, please go now." But she was touched by his move and struggling hard for words said, "And tell—your men—I am sorry that I spoke sharply to them. I—I am not quite myself today. Now, go."

He bowed, defeated yet grateful, and walked slowly back to the car. Kate followed him as if she did not know why. They looked at each other once more, she silent and her eyes beseeching.

"No," he replied to her pleading, questioning eyes, "No, I'm not going away until I know what is wrong. Call me if—if—" he stopped.

She nodded, unsmiling. He stepped into the car and drove away. Kate, standing there looking after him, suddenly found herself sobbing, not caring who knew, or why. Behind her on the terrace Lady Mary and Wells stood, the one shocked, the other vexed. Kate crying!

Why should Kate cry now when the Americans were gone at last?

"Kate," Lady Mary comamnded. "Kate, come here!"

But before Kate could comply, the screech of a bus rounding the corner into the park was heard. The first of three charabancs filled with tourists came sweeping up to the steps. The doors opened and people poured out.

Wells took up his position by the door to the castle. Kate sped to Lady Mary's side, slipping her hand through her arm. Lady Mary stood as if at attention, but the trippers had no eyes for her or if they did they said nothing. They had come to see a relic of ancient England and each one was determined to get his shilling's worth.

"Quaint little castle," someone said.

"It's one of England's oldest," another replied.

They went into the great hall and walked slowly about, looking at the tapestries on the walls, touching the paneling with admiring fingers.

"Silly little towers, I say," someone remarked.

"Norman," another answered, "or so the book says."

"How could people ever live in such moldy old places?" a woman asked.

"For reasons of their own," her husband answered.

"It's not like a house, is it, Mummie? It's more like a museum."

"That's about all castles are good for these days, and to teach children their history."

"It would give me the creeps to live here, fair give me the creeps."

"That's what I say, let's get out into the sunshine."

So the conversations went as the tide of curious, wide-eyed people flowed from room to room.

. . . Lady Mary and Kate were sitting on a bench under an ancient beech until they could enter the castle as their own again. Through the quiet of the drowsy afternoon came the sound of galloping hooves, then Sir Richard could be seen riding in from the direction of the village, and he was riding as if leading an army into battle. His right hand was held high. In it was a sword whose blade flashed in the sunlight. Kate, with Lady Mary clinging to her arm, hastened from their shelter. They reached the steps that led up to the west door as Sir Richard reined in his stallion before them. His face was flushed, his eyes wild, and he whirled the sword above their heads.

"Where is he?" he shouted. "Where is the foreigner? Where are his men?"

Wells hurried down the steps to lay his hands on the bridle of the horse.

They stared at Sir Richard with a strange mixture of terror and admiration. He made a picture there, on the panting horse, a portrait from another age, his splendid carriage, his powerful frame, the handsome head, the strong right arm swinging the sword.

"Oh, Wells," Lady Mary whispered, "isn't he glorious? My heart breaks—what shall I do? What shall I do?" Then she cried out, "Richard, where have you been?"

"Leave him to me, my lady," Wells whispered.

Gently he stroked the horse's nose. "He's all in a lather, Your Majesty," he said quietly. "You've come a long way, I daresay. But you can rest now—they've gone —all of them."

"Then I must go after them," Sir Richard cried. "I'll pursue them to the very end."

"It's no use, Richard," Lady Mary said. "Now, please get down from your horse and come in. We'll have tea. I'm sure you're famished."

He stared at her as though he did not know her. "Silence, woman! Into the castle! This is war—Lord Dunsten, your horse! Follow me—we'll find them—"

Kate had not stirred from where she stood. Was this a nightmare and in the middle of the afternoon? Why did her grandfather coax Sir Richard as though he knew what it was all about? And Lady Mary— "Oh, please," Kate moaned.

Then Sir Richard saw the three charabancs standing in the drive, and the people strolling across the terrace and into the garden. "They're attacking again!" he screamed. "They've come in full force!"

Now Kate ran to his side, and suddenly she knew exactly what to do. "Sir Richard, come down off your horse. We must go into the castle, all of us quickly, and lock the great gates. You're quite right. We are besieged."

He looked at her uncertainly. The people in the garden stared at them but went on with their tour.

"Come, come," Kate urged, "before they take the castle."

He responded at once. "To the throne room then," he shouted. "Meet me there, Lord Dunsten! Kate, help me— this sword—damned heavy—I daren't put it down."

She helped him dismount, Lady Mary standing by, the tears running down her cheeks, and they went into the castle, not by the great hall, filled with tourists, but by the side entrance, across the west terrace, into the library.

"Leave him to me," Kate whispered to Lady Mary. "I'll coax him to his room. . . . Grandfather, tell the people to go away again—he's ill, tell them—they'll have their money back—"

Wells nodded and she followed Sir Richard, taking his arm, letting him lean on her. He seemed lucid again for a moment or so she thought when they had reached his rooms.

"I've ridden a long way, Kate," he said in his usual voice. "There was some urgency it seemed—only what am I doing with this great sword?"

"I'll take it," she said.

He looked at her with sudden wild suspicion, a look of desperate fear.

He was someone else again.

"No, no—I'll not let it out of my hand. It's a trick—do you think I don't see it?"

She stood facing him, bewildered, and then to her horror, he pointed the sword at her and advanced toward her. She backed away from him until she was against the wall and could go no farther. She stared at him terrified, speechless. He stood over her, his eyes glaring under the brushy brows. Then he lowered the sword and a strange savage melancholy took the place of anger.

"My child," he muttered. "My child—my child—"

His voice was husky, his eyes suddenly tender, and she was only the more frightened.

"Don't," she gasped. "Don't hurt me!"

He shook his head, smiled, and laid the sword down on a table; then, seeming to forget her, he pressed the panel behind her. It slid back as she stepped aside. He entered the space it opened and the panel closed again. She caught her breath and then ran to find Lady Mary and tell her—tell her what? That Sir Richard had disappeared!

She found her back on the terrace, an indomitable figure of command, while Wells pushed the grumbling people into the waiting charabancs.

"The bloody aristocrats—"

"We'll report them, never fear—"

"Castle belongs to the public now, don't it?"

"A heap of rubble—that's all it is."

Kate went to Lady Mary. "Come, my dear," she said gently. "Come and have your tea, before you die of all this."

The dust stirred by the buses had scarcely settled when Philip Webster drove up in his small and noisy car. He was surprised to see Lady Mary with Kate beside her standing on the terrace, and Wells shaking his hands as if he could never free them of contamination.

"Then I'm not too late for tea?" Webster asked hopefully.

"No, no." Lady Mary's manner was always gracious when entertaining was in order. "As a matter of fact, we were just going in to make ourselves ready. It has been an unusual afternoon."

"Are you feeling better now, Lady Mary?"

"Certainly, Philip. I'm not sure that there was ever anything wrong with me. Where have you been and what have you been doing with yourself?"

"I've been on the telephone for hours, Lady Mary"— he spoke rapidly, nervously—"whenever I could get David Holt off it. My, my, how long-winded an American can be! I presented our case over again to all the top people, and they promised to look into it as soon as possible, which may mean next week or next year. I say, where's Sir Richard?"

"He is in the castle. I only hope he is all right," Lady Mary said as she led the way inside.

Wells disappeared in the direction of the kitchen muttering something about tea, while Kate walked beside Lady Mary.

"What, what?" Webster spluttered as they walked. "Is there another mystery?"

"Let us go and find him," Lady Mary said.

Kate spoke. "I think he'll be in his room, my lady."

"What about tea?" Webster complained.

They were deaf to the complaint and he could only follow Lady Mary and Kate. Somewhere along the passage Wells joined them unobtrusively. The door to Sir Richard's room was closed but not locked, and Kate opened it. Across the room the panel stood open again. Sir Richard had come back—ah, for the sword! It was gone from the table.

Lady Mary turned to Webster, her face gray, her voice cold. "Did you know about this panel, Philip?"

"Yes," Webster said. "It was his father's idea. This was always his room, you know, but when he died Sir Richard moved into it."

"I never knew that," Lady Mary said. "Nor did I know about this—this exit. Where does it lead?"

"To the east tower room," Webster replied. "I was there once. As a matter of fact, his father died in that room."

"That, too, I did not know," Lady Mary said.

"I knew, my lady," Wells put in. "I was there when he died. So was Sir Richard—a very young man he was then. The death came all of a sudden. His father was sitting in the big oaken chair that's still in the room. They were looking at a book—a biggish book, very old. It tells about the castle. Suddenly his father gave a loud sigh and fell forward, his head on the book. It was a fearful shock, though we knew his heart was bad ever since he was wounded so grievous. In the war. At Liège. He'd been joking with Sir Richard—the two of them were very close—almost mysterious—and he'd just said something about his son, the prince, and he raised his arm and waved an old silk flag that was folded into the book— Sedgeley coat of arms it was on the flag—and he sang out something like 'The King is dead—long live the King,' in French it was, and he was laughing. The very next minute he was dead."

"How much I've never known," Lady Mary whispered. Her white face was whiter than ever. She looked about the room vaguely. "Where is Kate? Tell her I—I—I must—"

"Here I am, my lady," Kate said, alarmed. "Shall you go back to your own room, dear?"

Lady Mary shook her head. "No. We must find him . . . in there. . . ."

She pointed to the open panel and again led the way, now into the passage beyond, Webster on one side, Kate

on the other and Wells behind. They walked in silence up
the ascending way until Wells spoke. "There was stairs
here once, my lady, but his father—Sir Richard's father
—had them made into a ramp, so he could walk more
easy-like."

No one replied. They walked on until they came to the
end, winding their way through the tower until they
reached the closed door at the top.

"I remember this," Lady Mary said. She tried the door
but it was bolted from the inside.

"Richard," she called. "Open the door, please."

They heard no sound except a strangled cough.

"Richard, open the door at once," she commanded.

Something fell to the floor. A chair moved—a heavy
chair.

"Let me talk to him, my lady," Wells said in a low
voice. He went close to the door and raised his voice.
"My liege, the enemy is defeated. We've routed them. I
am at your service, my liege!"

Sir Richard made instant reply in a great voice. "You
are a traitor, Lord Dunsten! It was you who allowed the
enemy to enter my castle! Call my guards!"

They listened, they looked at Wells. He shook his
head and began again bravely. "Your Majesty, you
wrong me—indeed you do! I served your father and I
serve you faithfully! But if you believe me guilty, I'll
call the guards—I'll give myself up!"

"Dismiss those persons who are with you," Sir Richard
shouted. "I will open the door but only to you."

Lady Mary nodded, she motioned to Kate and Webster
to follow her and they walked some feet away along the
passage and looked back at Wells. He stood for a long
moment, giving out great gusty sighs. He took a few steps
away, then returned again to the door. He folded his
arms, glanced at them, bowed to them as though in farewell, then gave seven knocks on the door.

They heard the sound of the bolt.

"Are you alone?" Sir Richard's voice echoed down the passage.

"Yes, my liege," Wells said in a loud voice.

"Have the horses saddled! You'll follow me."

"Saddle the horses!" Wells shouted, his high old voice cracking with effort. "His Majesty's orders! Americans to be routed!"

The door opened to reveal not Sir Richard but his right arm, holding the sword. Wells went in and the door closed with a slam.

Lady Mary held her breath until the door closed. Then she turned with sudden strength to Webster.

"Call the doctor," she said. "Tell him to come at once. We do not know what will happen behind that closed door—tell him there is no time to waste."

She walked rapidly down the passage toward the great hall.

Kate ran after her. "My lady," she gasped. "If you will excuse me for a moment—I've thought of something. Wait for me in the great hall, my lady."

She had indeed thought of something—John had said he was not leaving the village yet! She flew to the pantry telephone and called the inn. The innkeeper himself answered.

"Is Mr. Blayne there, George? This is Kate at the castle."

"He's here, all right, just sat down to a cup of tea in the garden. What's amiss? You're breathing like a grampus."

"I must speak to him, if you please," she cried. "A very important message, tell him."

"Well, I'll call him," George grumbled.

"Please, George," she begged. A moment or two later she heard his voice.

"John Blayne—"

"Oh," she cried, still breathless. "Please, will you go to America immediately?"

"Kate! What on earth?"

"Please, I can't say it on the telephone, what with the whole village listening in—but it's very dangerous for you. Don't delay at all, not a moment!"

He remonstrated. "Now really, Kate, this is too mysterious! If it's as dangerous as that, I shall come to the castle and see for myself."

"Indeed you must not!"

"Then tell me—"

"It's—it's that Sir Richard's not well—he's not himself. We don't know why—but he wants to—to—kill you."

He laughed. "Kill me? How absurd!"

"Ah, but he does! It's better if you never see him again. Believe me, better for all of us."

"Why should I be afraid?"

"He thinks you're his enemy."

He laughed again. "Nonsense—we're not living in the Middle Ages."

"Sir Richard is—and it's not for laughing, either, if it's me you're laughing at! I tell you he wants to kill you!"

"Kate—"

"Yes?"

"Are you afraid for *me?*"

Her voice came very small and hesitant. "Yes."

"Then I'm coming."

"No—please, please leave the village—leave England—pack your things now, at this moment—"

"Can't I wait until tomorrow just to see how he is?"

"No. It's life and death. Good-bye, good-bye."

"Good-bye, Kate," he said and hung up.

When he turned, the innkeeper was standing behind him.

"What was all that?" he inquired. "What's wrong at the castle, Mr. Blayne?"

"They want me out of the country," he said slowly. "I don't know why. I don't understand."

"When Sir Richard gives an order, he means it to be obeyed." The voice held a note of warning.

"Perhaps it depends on who receives the order."

"That Kate is a strong-minded lass, Mr. Blayne, but she's a good girl. Lady Mary is lucky to have such a maid in this day and age. Why, it's all I can do to get—"

"She's not a maid, George."

"What is she then?" George's round eyes grew rounder. "Who is she then?"

"I shall find out. That's why I'm staying."

"Shall you want a room here at the inn tonight, Mr. Blayne?"

John did not answer for a moment, then he nodded his head thoughtfully. "Perhaps I will, George, just for tonight, just in case."

"What will you be doing now, Mr. Blayne?"

"I'm going back to the castle as soon as I've finished my tea."

. . . In the tower room Wells was facing his master.

"Put down the sword, Your Majesty," he said.

Sir Richard, with the sword pointed at Wells, muttered thickly, "I'll run you through."

The room was dancing in circles through his bloodshot eyes, purple circles shot with brilliant lights. He could barely see Wells, a dim ghost in the whirling colors.

"I must open the door, my liege," Wells said. "Your queen must know everything now."

"I'll tell her myself, you traitor," Sir Richard roared. He advanced, searching for the gray figure that now was there and now was gone.

Suddenly he heard noises behind him—someone grunting and groaning, the shriek of a bolt in its rusty hasp. Wells had stepped behind him. He whirled about, nearly fell, and recovered himself. Wells had to sidestep, the door still fast shut.

"You devil!" he shouted. "You'd trick me, would you? You'd run to my enemies! I've a way to stop you at last. Richard the Fourth—I'll do what Richard the Third did —this sword—this sword—these damned colors floating everywhere! . . . Hah, but I see you there!"

He did indeed see a white and terrified face, the face of an old man, a stranger. He thrust the sword toward that face and even as he did so the body crumpled and fell to the floor. He saw a head at his feet and the sword in his hand. He stared down, bewildered.

"It's bloody," he muttered in disgust. He dropped the sword and it clattered on the stone floor.

. . . Outside the door the little group stood in the passage, listening in awe and terror. Nobody had come to help them. The doctor, Webster reported, was not in his office. The Americans had long since been dismissed.

"Should I not call the vicar, at least?" Kate was saying, and at that moment saw John, at the far end of the passage and running toward them.

"Oh, thank God, thank God," Lady Mary cried at sight of him. "Only, how did you know that we needed help?"

"Kate told me not to come—some sort of danger— so, of course, I came. I went straight to Sir Richard's room and that panel was open—I simply went through it and kept going like the White Rabbit in *Alice in*—" He broke off at the sight of their faces. "Tell me quickly," he demanded, suddenly grave.

"Sir Richard is in there." Lady Mary gestured. "He's bolted the door."

"My grandfather is in there, too," Kate said and stopped.

"Sir Richard is very ill," Webster said. "We must find a way to reach him."

"The dungeon," Kate exclaimed. "There's a passage—"

"The door to it is solid iron," Lady Mary reminded her. "And it's locked."

"There'll be a key somewhere," Webster said. "The lock will be rusty, of course, but if there was a hatchet—"

"Yes," Kate told him. "Sir Richard's father had it put in for the wine cellars."

"If the door's iron—" Webster began but John cut him short.

"One of my men had an electric drill with him, he was coming back tomorrow to get it."

He turned quickly and sped back through the passage, Kate after him. By the time Lady Mary and Webster could reach the dungeon door they heard the sound of the electric drill cutting through the metal. The machine made hideous noises and it was impossible to speak. They could only wait.

"Now," John said at last, "help me, Webster. This door is heavy and we must let it fall easily. Lucky it's narrow! Kate, take this machine away. Now then, Webster—you on that side. I'll take this. Stand back, please, Lady Mary."

They obeyed him without a word. Together he and Webster lowered the door slowly to the stone floor. They peered into the darkness beyond and saw a windowless cell. John stepped over the threshold.

"It's a shaft," he exclaimed. "Look, Webster—there's no ceiling. I see a square of light at the top."

Webster went in and stared upward. "You're right—it leads up the tower."

"How to get there," John mused. "There must be steps—yes—in the wall here. Can you feel them?"

"Good God, yes," Webster exclaimed. "But I'd hate to—"

"Do you hear a voice?" Lady Mary called.

"Not even a whisper," John answered. He was searching the steps carved into the rock. "I can climb. I'll climb up and see—what—"

"Oh no!" It was Kate, pressing into the shaft. "Oh please, don't climb up there. If you fall—"

"I shan't fall," John said. "I'm a mountain climber, Kate—a good one."

He was already beginning to climb, clinging with his hands to the step above him, feeling his way.

"Oh, but what will happen to you when you get there?" she cried, wringing her hands. "How do you know—"

"The only way to know is to find out. Take Lady Mary upstairs. Obey me, Kate—Webster, go with them. I'll meet you at the top when I get that door open."

They obeyed again and alone he climbed slowly but skillfully the shallow steps. The square opening at the top was, he surmised, a trapdoor. He remembered such a door in the old stables of his childhood home in Connecticut. Then he had climbed through tunnels of hay. Now he climbed through rock, trying not to think, determined not to be afraid. The silence was unearthly, not a voice, not a sound. Where was Sir Richard?

Endlessly he climbed, trying to make no noise. Once on the edge of a step his hand slipped and he was all but catapulted to the bottom of the shaft, but he caught himself on the step above. Hand over hand, one foot after the other, he felt his way to the opening and pulled himself through the trapdoor and into the room. It was ablaze with light from a lamp set on a carved oak table. He tried to shut the trapdoor, but it would not fold back on its ancient hinges.

Someone was sitting at the table in a great oaken chair, a strange figure wrapped in an old robe of purple velvet, and wearing a gold crown—no, a crown of gold tinsel. Sir Richard! It could not be and yet he knew instantly that it was. He was mumbling over a book, an enormous book, and he was holding something in his right hand, resting one end on the floor. A scepter? It looked the real thing. Heavy with gold and glittering with encrusted jewels! There was this much treasure then. Sir Richard had found it. Why in heaven's name was he hiding it here? What was the mystery?

John stood alone by the trapdoor. Should he speak? He must speak—

"Sir Richard," he said gently.

Sir Richard lifted his head as though to listen, and without answer let it fall again as though he had not heard. Then John saw what lay beside the door, the crumpled body of Wells! Beside it was a sword, a long, thin blade, and, he saw to his horror, it was still shining wet with blood.

He stood in shock, staring at the sight. Sir Richard was mumbling again, his head sunken on his breast. What could be done? John wondered. Certainly he must not rouse him until the door was opened. He remained motionless, endeavoring to see whether the bolt of the door was still shot into the hasp. Bolt? There were three bolts! All bolts were shot, the door still barred. He must creep to it without a sound and draw the bolts back one after the other, and so throw the door open. But the sword—he must take that, for safety, and keep it near him.

Holding his breath, his eyes upon Sir Richard, he reached the door and put out his hand across the dead body. Poor Wells! He looked away from the dead face set in a grimace of fear, the open eyes. . . . The first bolt drew easily without a sound. The second bolt made a slight screech. The mumbling stopped. He stood motionless for an instant and then turned to look behind him. Sir Richard had not moved. He still sat with his head bent above the book, seeing nothing and yet intent on the open page.

But he was silent! Were his eyes closed? It might be that he had fallen into a doze. He waited, watching—perhaps Sir Richard was asleep, the light sleep of the aged. He must make haste. He tried to draw the third bolt back. It was stiff and would not yield easily. He had to use both hands and all his strength. The bolt was not half drawn when he felt something at his back, something sharp and pressing. He glanced backward toward his right. The sword was gone from the floor. He knew instantly whose hand held it.

"Sir Richard," he said distinctly. "I am here only to help you."

At this the sword pressed more deeply, forcing him to move toward the left, and yet he could not escape it. However he moved, Sir Richard held the sword into his back, cutting through his clothes, he could now feel, and pricking his skin.

"I wanted this meeting," Sir Richard muttered through his clenched teeth. "I sought it! This settles everything between us after all these years, now you are in my power. After all these years—pursuing me—"

"Sir Richard, recall yourself," John urged. He was being pushed step by step toward the trapdoor, the sword in his back.

"Forcing me to hide my son to save his life—in vain—in vain! Your bombs killed him."

Son? What son? Sir Richard had no son. A dream of a son never born!

He felt a stab of pain and a warm trickle down his back.

"Sir Richard! I am your friend," he cried desperately. "You can't hate a friend—come now!"

"I do not deign to hate you," Sir Richard retorted. "And call me by my proper name! What I do is my duty as a king. I could have had you poisoned while you sat at my table. But that would have burdened others. This task I must perform alone. To your knees, to your knees—"

For John had twisted himself suddenly up and now the two faced each other. . . . Good God, the absurdity of this, that he should be at the mercy of a mad old Englishman! Yet here he was, pinned between the point of a sword and a trapdoor. He had been a good fencer at Harvard. Once in his freshman year he had caught a sword in his hand, and he knew how fierce a weapon a sword was.

"To your knees, I tell you!" Sir Richard was shouting. "I'll teach you how to show yourself before a king!"

"Now, please . . ." John began. He tried to laugh but laughter died in his throat. Those eyes, glaring at him with maniacal fury, impossible . . . to . . .

"Down on your knees!" Sir Richard ground the words between his teeth.

He slipped to his knees to escape the sword. "Sir Richard—listen to me! All right—king, whatever you are—Lady Mary was right—there is a treasure—it's on the table yonder—your royal scepter—a king's ransom—you'll keep your castle. Put down your sword. You don't need it, I tell you. I'll call Lady Mary and tell her you are waiting for her with the treasure—the treasure, man!"

Sir Richard was staring at him, but the fury was fading. He looked puzzled. His right hand dropped, he went to the table uncertainly and putting down the sword, he took up the scepter.

John stood upright again and edged his way toward the table and the sword, still talking.

"Webster will know how to dispose of the scepter—it's a fortune in itself."

He reached for the sword. Ah, thank God, he was in control now. He could open the door and get help; but he had no sooner grasped the sword than he saw Sir Richard lift the heavy scepter high in both hands and to his amazement prepare to bring it down on his head, as though it were a mace. He stepped back and thrust the sword in fencing position to fend him off, feinting this way and that, diverting each blow that Sir Richard dealt, but by so narrow a margin that he knew he could not relent for the fraction of a second. He saved himself once by leaping aside as the scepter glittered above his head. It fell then on a corner of the oaken table and split it off.

And while the mad duel went on, he trying not to wound Sir Richard but only to save his own life, he was aware, though dimly, of a constant muttering in his ears, a gasping groaning stream of broken talk pouring from Sir Richard's foaming mouth.

"His body ashes—my son, my son! Wells knew. Where's Wells? Wells—Wells—Wells—"

Sir Richard's voice rose to a shriek and he lifted the scepter again, high over his head, and staggered forward.

Out of the welter of words John heard the scream and dared not pause. The scepter was above his head. He feinted and darted right and left, escaping from corner to corner. Sir Richard pursued him erratically, managing somehow to pin him at one side or the other, using the scepter like a club. Once it skinned his cheek, once it struck his left arm, now it fell on his shoulder. Ah, but the sword was strong, a gem of a sword, as he could tell, and his hand had not lost its cunning. Sir Richard played for strength and he for skill, he in silence trying not to wound his opponent, and Sir Richard gasping and muttering beneath the scepter's weight. Scepter and sword locked. They were face to face and Sir Richard hissed in his face.

"You want my scepter. I know you. I know your sort.

Smooth tongue . . . black heart . . . traitors, all of you. I'll brain you. That sword's mine . . . my father's sword . . . put it down . . . I'll deal with you as I did with Dunsten. I trusted him . . . these years . . . raised him from a commoner . . . the only one who had my confidence. I . . . I . . . gave him my son . . . my only son . . . told him my secret. How else could he have got a wife like her? He let her die in childbirth. Killed her, likely. And then let them kill my son. There's only a girl left . . . no heir . . . a girl . . ."

He heard these groans, these mutterings, his ears alert and his mind whirling with what they meant. This mystery, this hidden secret story. And the man gone mad with fear at the thought of losing all he had. Oh, who was Kate? Would he ever know, now that Wells was dead?

"Fool," Sir Richard was saying between clenched teeth. "I've been the fool—thinking myself safe because I had the castle . . . all these wild peoples rising everywhere in the world . . . British lion—the castle's besieged . . . lost. They're coming . . . I see them . . . I see them . . . I give my life . . ."

He lifted the scepter high above his head again, his arms trembling under its weight, and charged at John, forcing him back, back toward the trapdoor.

"Down—down!" he bellowed. "Down where traitors belong!"

"Take care—for yourself!" John cried.

His feet caught on the edge of the trapdoor. He thrust the sword upward to ward off the descending weapon. The scepter fell on the sword, the blade broke at the hilt. He was flung to one side by the impact. He rolled on the floor, ducking like a football player. Sir Richard, unable to save himself, was hurled head first into the trapdoor.

John Blayne crawled to the door, dazed, his head aching from the blow, the broken sword still in his right hand. The body of Wells lay there, unmoved by all the strife. With his left hand John put the limbs gently aside so that he could open the door. Still clutching the broken sword, scarcely knowing that he did so, he worked the last bolt from its hasp and opened the door.

They were waiting outside and they stared at him.

Kate cried out at sight of him. "You're bleeding!"

She snatched the little ruffled apron from about her waist and ran to him and began wiping his face, talking all the while. "We heard the most dreadful—oh, John— such a bruise! How did it happen? And you with the sword broken—"

"Where is Sir Richard?"

It was Lady Mary, standing in the doorway, her eyes searching the room. She pushed her way in and saw the body on the floor.

"Oh Richard," she whispered. "Oh no— How could you, how could you . . ."

Now she saw the scepter. She went to it, took it up and dropped it as though it burned her hands. For there before her the hole gaped and he was nowhere . . . nowhere . . .

She turned, her eyes searching, uncomprehending, until they rested on John. She stood looking at him, trying to speak. When her voice came it was a whisper, a gasp.

"Take this castle away. Take it . . . it's evil. I always knew it was. It's full of . . . ghosts." She swayed, and caught herself and stood leaning against the table, her face white and cold.

"Kate, take care of her!" John cried.

But Lady Mary pushed them all away when they came to her side.

"I am quite all right," she said. She tried to moisten her lips, her mouth dry. She turned to them with a wild sad smile, her haunted eyes unseeing.

"*They* were no help at all—no help! So perhaps *they* simply don't exist!"

This she said in her high clear voice, and repulsing the hands stretched out to help her, she walked away from them all.

. . . The day was cool, the air clear with the delicate sunshine of an English morning in summer. The castle had never been more beautiful, John thought. He had strolled up from the village, needing time to be alone before he met Kate. The landscape was still and calm, the village too had been silent. People stayed in their houses, talking quietly of the shadow that had fallen upon the countryside. The inquest had been held—accidental death. So Sir Richard was dead, the last of the Sedgeleys, and who was to have the castle now? John had ordered his breakfast sent to his room, but Thomas had waylaid him at the door.

"What will we all be doing now, sir?" he asked. "We looked up to Sir Richard, you know, sir. Fussy he was at times, and a man of his own mind, but we was used to that from him and his father. High and mighty, but they'd a right to be. The likes of them made old England. So what's to happen to us?"

"I don't know, Thomas," he said. "I don't think anybody knows just yet. But you'll be told, doubtless."

"We'll have to wait," Thomas said dolefully.

John had nodded and gone his way along the cobbled road to the edge of the village, and then the country road through the meadows and the wood. Kate would be waiting for him in the yew walk. Last night when he had seen to it that all was arranged for the funeral today, they had clasped hands at parting.

"I'll come in the morning," he had promised. "I'll meet you in the yew walk—about eleven?"

She had nodded.

Yes, he could see her figure now—a white dress, in the shadowy walk. How small she looked between the great shrubs towering darkly above her! The sunlight fell straight and she walked in a path of sunlight, narrow, but wide enough for her to escape the shadows, and her hair was bright in the sunshine.

They met, he held both her hands in his and restrained himself from taking her in his arms. It was still too soon. She was grave from all that had happened.

"The vicar's here," she said. "He came early. Lady Mary sent for him. She wants the crypt to be full of red roses. She won't have a long sermon, she says. And the people are to be allowed to come in and stand as close as they like—and the broken sword is to be put back into its place."

"How is she?" John asked.

"Brave," Kate said. "She talked about him this morning quite calmly, though I'm sure she hadn't slept—such deep shadows under her pretty eyes. She said she was glad he had gone first, because she could bear being alone better than he could; because women are stronger about some things, she said. Men want so much, she told me—but we women ask very little, really. Just someone to give us a little affection, someone to talk to—and a hand to hold—"

Her voice broke. He took her in his arms. She leaned her head on his breast, and he laid his cheek against her hair.

"Kate—" he said after a moment.

"Yes, John?"

"I'm not coming to the funeral. Will she mind too much? I can't—after that last dreadful meeting in the throne room."

They paused, still holding hands, and he looked into her upturned face, flawless in the sunlight.

"No," Kate said. "She'll understand—a wonderfully understanding woman. She said this morning she wished she hadn't to go to the funeral, either. She stayed with him alone yesterday evening. She said she was glad he was peaceful at last with his ancestors, where he'd always belonged."

He wondered, watching her, if Lady Mary had told her anything of herself. Did Kate know that she was the daughter of Sir Richard's son, and so his own granddaughter?

"Kate, look at me!"

She obeyed instantly, lifting her face to his, and meeting his smile she blushed sweetly.

"Yes, John?"

"Has Lady Mary ever said anything to you about a child?"

"A child? No, John. What child?"

Kate was thinking, remembering. "She did say she wished so much she could have given Sir Richard a child. She said it was her fault they hadn't an heir. But I told her it wasn't, because she wanted a child as much as he did—a son, of course, for the castle."

"What did she say then?"

"She said there was no use in talking about it. And then, I don't know why, she told me that Queen Elizabeth came here to this castle after Essex was beheaded. She loved him, you know, though he was half her age, but she said nothing after he was dead. Her motto had always been *Video et taceo*. And it was a good motto for a woman, Lady Mary said, especially for a woman who loves a man."

"*I see and I am silent*," John repeated. "It's a good motto for us all."

A silence fell between them.

"You don't want the castle now, I suppose," Kate said. She pulled her hands away as she spoke and tucked them into the pockets of her dress.

He answered slowly, pausing often to reflect. "It would be easy for me to run away from it, run away and forget. Yes, the castle fills my heart with horror, and with love. It's an old, old castle. . . . Even castles must have evil in them when they live too long. But it isn't the castle that's evil, it's the people who used it for evil. See how the sunlight falls there on the towers, Kate? See how beautiful it is?"

He drew her with him and they looked between the yews. "It's a work of art. I don't want it destroyed, any more than I want a book or a painting ruined. I want generations of people—new generations—to enjoy it, and purify it through new life."

"And you're taking it away?"

"Yes, I think that's been settled legally and voluntarily," he said, "but I'll leave something in its place— a fine modern farm, the best of machinery. My father will like that! And Lady Mary will live nearby and see the earth bloom—"

"And I'll be staying with her," Kate said in a low voice.

"You're wrong," he said firmly. "She won't let you. If I know her, and I think I do—ah, but I'm sure I do— she won't let you. And I won't let you. You'll live on the other side of the ocean, in a new country, my little Kate. With the man who loves you."

She drew a deep breath, then tried to laugh. "How you can be so sure of—of everything!" she cried. "How you can tell it all out like that!"

He took her face between his hands. "You tell me," he said. "Am I right?"

A long look passed between them—no, much more than a look. He saw through those violet eyes straight and deep into her heart, and she looked up and saw what she wanted to see, a man she could adore and did, and did—

"Yes!" she said.

"And shall we go on living in the castle," she inquired, "after it's moved to Connecticut?"

"No," he said firmly. "We will not live in it. Nobody will live in it, ever again. We'll live in a new house, you and I, and there'll be a wing in it for Lady Mary, if she likes the idea of a new country, another life—without ghosts—"

"Oh," she breathed in ecstasy. "How you do think of everything!"

They kissed then, for what else was there to do after that, and drew apart at last and only because the church bells were tolling. No, they were ringing.

"Hark," Kate whispered. "Lady Mary said they weren't to toll. They're ringing a song he used to sing with her when they were young—it's what she told them to do. 'I won't have the smell of death, nor the sound of it,' that's what she told the vicar. . . ."

She hesitated and gave him a coaxing smile. "But I'll just go and be with her a bit, John, shan't I? Until this is over? Since I'm to have the rest of my life with you?"

How could he refuse her, now or ever?

He nodded, smiling, and sat down on a garden seat, from where over the dark yews he could see the castle towering against the blue sky.

"I'll wait," he said.